DESCENT

into

MADNESS

Praise for the Thomas Martindale Mysteries

Murder at Yaquina Head

"Wry, thoughtful, moody, and structured around a secret that reaches back to the era of World War II, *Murder at Yaquina Head* is a 183-page, gripping mystery which is highly recommended for mystery buffs and would make a welcome and appreciated addition to any community library."

—*The Bookwatch*

". . . good stuff for a mystery. What really makes it a good read, however, is the self-effacing Martindale, a delightful if sometimes exasperating sleuth who is far too nosy for his own good." —*Denver Post*

". . . Lovell's firsthand knowledge lends an air of credibility to the story and the setting. . . . He crafts a convincing story peppered with absorbing details about World War II." —*Booklist*

Dead Whales Tell No Tales

"It always seems a little strange to say that a murder mystery is fun. But sometimes they are. Ron Lovell's second venture into the mystery field is a good example. This is a solid mystery with good characters and deft writing."

—*Statesman Journal*

"*Dead Whales* is a compelling who-done-it that will keep you guessing until the very last chapter. The characters feel very real—as well intended and as flawed as the people around us every day. It is a pleasure to read author Ron Lovell's well-crafted prose." —Clinton McKinzie, author of *Crossing the Line*

"An excellent read from an accomplished writer."

—*Midwest Book Review*

Murder Below Zero

"The author is skilled at ratcheting up suspense while moving Martindale and company into deeper and deeper doo-doo. Nasty revelations and dashed hopes terrorize the expedition members and keep readers turning the pages. . . . Although the book's cover describes it as a 'mystery,' Lovell's storytelling has more in common with Tom Clancy than Agatha Christie."

—*Fairbanks Daily News-Miner*

A Thomas Martindale Mystery

DESCENT

into

MADNESS

Ron Lovell

Ron Lovell

A Penman Productions Book

Printed in the United States of America
Library of Congress Control Number: 2007924941
ISBN: 978-0-9767978-5-2

Cover and book designer: Liz Kingslien
Editor: Mardelle Kunz
Cover photo: istock.com © Stefan Klein
Back cover photo: Linda Hosek

Penman
PRODUCTIONS

P.O. Box 400, Gleneden Beach, Oregon 97388
www.martindalemysteries.com

Special thanks to Dennis Wolverton for giving me such a good tour of the wilds of eastern Oregon.

Thanks to Jo Anne Trow, a longtime friend and colleague, for arranging a tour of the real Horner Museum. Contributions in support of the Horner Collection can be made to the Benton County Historical Society, P.O. Box 35, Philomath, Oregon 97370. The Society has acquired the Horner Collection and plans to exhibit many of its artifacts in its museum.

There is no great genius
without some touch of madness.

—Seneca

June 22, 2005

I had the kind of night where your mind is in such a turmoil that you don't think you've slept at all. First, there was the noise—incessant yelling and banging on the iron bars by inmates in the cells near mine. The hard, steel cot did not help matters, either; the thin pad over it did nothing for my back. I doubted I would ever be able to stand straight again. Luckily, I had been placed in a cell by myself, so I didn't have to worry about my personal safety. Then there was the worry. I had been arrested for murder, and I had no idea what to do. Thoughts of paying for a defense and putting my life and my career as a university professor back together filled my head to the bursting point.

But morning did come at long last.

At first light, I could actually see the blue sky through the skylight above my cell. Although I was still in deep denial about what had happened the day before, I knew I had to pull myself together, get out of this horrible place, and figure out how to clear my name.

1

I did not kill Maxine March. Anyone who knew me could not possibly believe that I would be capable of such a heinous act. Hell, I cared for Maxine. Maybe I even loved her. I could never do her any harm.

The events of the day before seemed to paralyze my brain. I was in a kind of dream that I hoped I would wake up from so I could go on with my privileged life. When I was put in this cell yesterday afternoon, I just curled up in a fetal position and let my mind go into a catatonic state—I was oblivious to the world around me.

I felt differently this morning. I was still in a world of trouble, but I knew I would not get out of it by lying here feeling sorry for myself. Even close friends could not help me. I would have to fight on my own to get my life back.

Creakily, I got up from the bunk and hobbled to the sink. My fifty-plus-year-old body felt as if it had been hit by a log truck. I bent over and splashed my face with water. I rinsed out my mouth the same way. Where did a guy get a toothbrush and toothpaste around here?

"Guard," I called through the small opening in the door.

Nothing.

"GUARD!" I raised my voice.

"Who's that?"

"Martindale. I'm at the end!"

Soon, the face of a sheriff's deputy appeared in the small opening. He was young and looked friendly. He also had a full head of hair, which softened his features. I noticed the day before that most of the deputies who worked in the jail had what I thought of as bullet heads—so clean-shaven they looked as if they had been polished. They were nice enough, but the absence of hair made them look tough and authoritarian.

"Mr. Martindale," the young deputy said cheerfully. "What can I do for you? You want something to eat?"

"Good morning . . . ," I caught his name on the tag on his uniform, "Deputy Sloan. I'm hungry, but first I need to make a phone call. I've seen enough TV shows to know that I get one call. Am I right?"

"That's one thing all those shows and movies got right. Yes, you do. Kind of early, though, to find anybody in an office. I mean, you calling a lawyer?"

"I am. I probably should have done it last night when I got in here, but I wasn't thinking very well. What time is it?"

"Almost 7 A.M. I'll get you the phone if you want to try now."

"Thanks, I think I will. I'll at least get his voice mail."

"Okay, I'll get the phone, and then I'll get some breakfast for you." Sloan returned in seconds with a telephone and handed it through the opening. "You could come into the hall and do it at the pay phone, but I'll bet you'd like some privacy."

"I would. Thanks. It's long distance, but I'll use my phone card."

Sloan walked back down the hallway, and I picked up the phone. It had no dial, but I was immediately connected to an operator.

"Collect or charge to another number?" asked the bored-sounding operator.

"Phone card."

"Speak up, I can hardly hear you. You people need to speak up."

"I said, I will charge this to a phone card."

"You don't have to shout," she said.

I did not need this kind of hassle, but I ignored her rudeness. I was sure that I was not the first inmate she had given a hard time to. I was trying to keep my voice down so others near my cell wouldn't hear what I was saying—I had not yet learned the lesson of being in jail: there was no privacy. I put the receiver close to my mouth and gave her my card number, which I had long ago memorized.

"What number do you wish to call?" Miraculously, she had

heard the number the first time. I didn't relish having my card used by the guys in nearby cells who doubtless would have many calls to make.

"I need information, then I'll get them to connect my call."

"Connecting you to Oregon information. Have a nice day."

Fat chance of that in here.

"Thanks."

Oregon information came on the line quickly, and I asked for the phone number of Lorenzo Madrid in Salem. I had been impressed with his skills as the defense attorney for Hector Morales, a man who had been on trial for murder the year before and whose jury I was thrown off by Madrid. Later, when I went to see him to find out more about Morales and his longtime patron, Duncan Delgado, I remember being impressed by his intelligence and character. He normally handled poor and illegal Mexican migrants, however, so I was not sure he would take my case.

Morales had turned up dead a day before Maxine's murder. I suspected Delgado in both slayings, but doubted anyone would believe me. Delgado was a biology professor on the faculty of the same university I was; he was also extremely clever and had outmaneuvered me at every turn. Maybe Madrid would be an exception.

The attorney himself answered the phone. "Caesar Chavez Legal Foundation."

"Mr. Madrid, you may not remember me. It's Tom Martindale. We met earlier this year. I was the one you threw off Hector Morales's jury."

"I remember you very well, Professor Martindale. What can I do for you?"

"I'm in a bit of a jam. As a matter of fact, I'm in jail and I need you to get me out."

* * * * *

Madrid took charge immediately and said he would handle everything. He told me not to talk to anyone about the case and said he would see me this afternoon. I felt relieved, although a bit worried about getting bail and how I could raise the money to pay it. And then there was the matter of Madrid's fee. He did not mention it, so I avoided that topic, too—for now.

After breakfast and a visit to the bathroom, I sat on my bed to think about what kind of money I could raise quickly. I did not own my condo in Corvallis, but my small house in Newport was free and clear of any debt. Although I was not sure how it worked, I figured I could put it up as collateral for the bond needed to pay the bail. Madrid would know what to do.

About three hours later, the young deputy was back at the small opening in the door to my cell. "You've got a visitor, Mr. Martindale." Who would have access to the jail, whose rules never allowed anyone in the cells except staff? Maybe it was Angela Pride. Things had been awkward between us lately, especially since she had to arrest me the day before.

"Is it a policewoman? She's a good—" The door opened, and I stood up with a smile on my face.

"Sorry to disappoint you, professor. I can't tell you how good it is to see you again, especially in such cozy circumstances."

Sheriff Art Kutler was an old nemesis from the coast. We had had a number of run-ins over the years, the first of which resulted in his being tossed out of office by voters because of something I did to him involving a beached whale. He blamed me for what happened even though he had been the guy who tried to blow up the carcass. Did I know there would be a cameraman nearby? And that the footage would create a sensation in Portland and in other TV markets around the country?

He walked into the cell and sat down on my bunk. He looked older, although his fat face had kept the wrinkles at bay. His belly still protruded over his Tom Brown belt as it always had.

"You know, professor, I always knew you would wind up this way. I tried to nail you for lots of things over the years, but you always slipped away. I'm glad somebody finally caught up with you. It's a sight to behold—I had to see you in here with my own eyes." Kutler was smiling broadly now. In fact, he seemed about to rub his hands together in absolute glee.

"Sheriff, I thought you'd died and gone to whatever heaven someone like you can hope to get into." I smiled back, deciding that politeness would not work with this small-minded, idiotic man.

"As a God-fearing Christian, I don't have to worry about where I'm goin'," he smirked. "You, on the other hand, had better start prayin'."

"To what do I owe the honor of this visit, sheriff? Need someone to write your life story? Let's see, we can call it *Memoirs of a Whale of a Sheriff*." Now it was my turn to smirk—and I did. His smile vanished.

"You shut up about that! I was doing my duty, and you had to interfere in your own superior way. You set me up, and I paid dearly for what you did. I don't forget little favors like that. You'd better be . . ."

"Are you browbeating my client, sheriff?"

Lorenzo Madrid stepped into the cell looking like a million dollars. He had on a gray double-breasted, pinstriped suit with a gleaming white shirt and a bright yellow tie. A matching handkerchief protruded out of the coat pocket and his shirt cuffs were equidistant from the sleeves of his coat. His perfectly jelled hair and gleaming white teeth set off his handsome face.

A look of fear crossed Kutler's face as it always did when he came up against someone who was obviously more intelligent than he was.

"I . . . er . . . I was just visiting an old friend. The professor and I . . . we go back a long way," said Kutler, looking even more rumpled next to the resplendent Madrid.

"I'm sure you do, sheriff, but visits from friends are not permitted in this jail. Am I right, deputy?"

The young deputy nodded, looking a bit sheepish at having been caught breaking the rules for a fellow lawman. I didn't want to make an issue of it. I liked this kid, and I didn't want him replaced with one of the bullet heads.

"I'll be getting on my way. I was just here to transport a prisoner. Want to join us, professor? I think you've been in our nice jail in Newport before."

"Sheriff." Madrid raised his hand and hooked his thumb toward the door. "We won't keep you. And stay away from my client. Agreed?"

Kutler mumbled something as he left the cell rather hastily; the deputy closed the door as he also left. Madrid sat down next to me on the cot, and we shook hands.

"Glad to see you, Mr. Martindale."

"Please. Make it Tom. We're going to be very good friends, I hope."

"You bet. And my name's Lorenzo. Okay, let's get right to it. I got your bail hearing set for four this afternoon. I know Judge Andrews pretty well, and I guess you know her, too."

I nodded. "Yeah, I talked to her once about the Morales case, and she arraigned me yesterday."

"Right. We need to get into that in a minute, but I want to talk about the steps we need to follow today to get you out of here. Not the worst jail I've seen, but not anything you're used to, I would guess."

"No kidding. I've been in jails and prisons to do stories, but never on this side of the bars. It hasn't been much fun, although I've been treated fairly. Somebody got me in this cell by myself.

That lowered my stress level a lot."

"Now we will need to post bail. You'll need to give the bondsman ten percent of the total. Let's say it's $250,000. Can you come up with $25,000 in a hurry?"

"I can turn over the title of my house in Newport," I said. "I've got maybe $15,000 in savings and another $10,000 in a CD."

"I didn't think professors made that much money," he said, smiling.

"It comes from being old and fairly conservative in how I spend money. I do some writing on the side and have saved a lot of the proceeds. Also, I'm an only child, and I got a small inheritance from my parents when they died."

"Okay, great. I will go right to the bail bondsman when I leave you. I have worked with him for years, and he owes me a favor or two. Give me the keys to your house and tell me where your house papers are. Also, I need to get you some decent clothes."

"The deputy can probably get you my keys. I turned over everything when I was booked."

Madrid nodded and stood up. We shook hands again.

"How can I thank you enough? You don't know me, but you've rushed down here to help me anyway. I . . . I don't know how I can repay you." My eyes filled with tears.

Madrid waved his hand to dismiss what I said. "You just tell me everything you know, and we'll get this cleared up. We'll get your gringo ass out of here pronto!" Madrid smiled as he saw my surprise at what he said. "I'm not so long out of the barrio that I've forgotten how my people talk there. I'll be back in a few hours. Leave it all to me."

As the door of the cell slammed behind him, I intended to do just that.

Thirty hours had made some difference in my attitude as I once again entered the Benton County Courthouse. With Lorenzo Madrid at my side, I felt a lot better about my prospects than I had the day before with a hapless public defender championing my case. For the first time since this whole mess started, I had some hope that this terrible misunderstanding could be cleared up.

Madrid had done an amazing amount of work in a few hours. He had gone to my condo and picked out a suit and shirt and tie. My blue pinstripe with matching accoutrements was left at the front counter of the jail. I washed up a bit, but did not take a shower. I shaved with a razor provided by the friendly deputy. My shoes were a bit too sporty for the rest of my outfit, but I doubted anyone would notice.

I still had to be led into court wearing shackles and handcuffs, but I pretended not to notice them. When I turned around to allow the bailiff to unlock the latter, I was relieved to see few people in the courtroom. I did not recognize anyone, nor were any television people present. One man, taking notes, was probably from the local newspaper. This lack of attention was fine with me. I would prefer to be a one-day story rather than one that continued for a week or longer.

Madrid smiled in a reassuring way and shook my hand, then motioned for me to sit in the chair next to him. "You clean up well," he whispered. "I think we are going to be okay. Just sit back and speak only when you are spoken to. You do not strike me as a hothead, so I know I can trust you to leave this up to me."

"I'm very happy to do that. Did you have any luck with the bail guy?"

"Just leave it up to me."

I nodded.

"All rise." The clerk had walked through the door at the front of the courtroom followed by the judge, whose black robes rustled as she made her way up onto the bench. "The circuit court is now in session. The Honorable J. Betty Andrews presiding."

The judge looked directly at me. "Please be seated. We're here to act on the bail request by defendant Thomas Martindale. I am ready to hear your motions. Mr. Bates."

The same rumpled assistant D.A. who had been at my arraignment stood up. "George Bates for the state, Your Honor. The state opposes bail of any kind. This may become a capital case. Mr. Martindale is charged with murdering a woman . . . ," he looked at his notes, ". . . a . . . er . . . a Maxine March, a fifty-five-year-old resident of Benton County, Oregon."

I wanted to leap to my feet and shout my innocence, but I remained seated and quiet.

"The evidence we will present at trial shows an intimate relationship between the defendant and the late Ms. March and then a severing of that relationship. The state considers that motive enough for this heinous act."

I grabbed Madrid's arm, but he sloughed me off.

"Save the characterization of what went on for trial, Mr. Bates," said the judge. "Anything else?"

"Nothing further, Your Honor."

Madrid stood up. "Lorenzo Madrid, for the defense."

The judge nodded at my attorney.

"The defense will not dignify the D.A.'s remarks with a reply delineating their fallaciousness. No such relationship existed. The defense asks that the defendant be release on his own recognizance."

Bates leaped to his feet. "We object, Your Honor. This is a murder case. We cannot sanction releasing murderers onto the street. The public good would be ill served by such an action."

"I am well aware of the seriousness of the charge, Mr. Bates. Please sit down. Mr. Madrid, you may continue."

Madrid smiled, seeming to have picked up some feeling of sympathy from the judge. I felt it, too. "The defendant is a respected member of the community, both the city as a whole and the university that forms its heart. He has never been in the slightest trouble with the law. He has never even gotten a parking ticket."

Bates snickered and shook his head vigorously until the judge's frown caused him to stop.

"This is a misunderstanding and, I might add, a possible misuse of the power of the police to arrest and detain a person."

"That is for a trial jury to decide," shouted Bates, again jumping to his feet.

"Mr. Bates, please sit down. Mr. Madrid, this is not the time to present your case. I need to know your reasons for asking your client's release on bail, nothing more."

"Sorry, Your Honor. Sometimes my determination to help the wrongfully accused be treated fairly causes me to overreact."

"You can say that again," muttered Bates.

"Mr. Bates, please."

"Sorry, Your Honor."

"Along with my client's exemplary record as a citizen and a public servant comes our contention that the body found by police several days ago may not be that of Maxine March."

The judge looked shocked, and Bates again leapt to his feet. "An outrageous falsehood!" he shouted. "There is absolutely no evidence to support this claim. Police recovered identification proving that Ms. March was the decedent found near the bridge."

"I presume DNA samples were gathered and processed?" said Madrid.

"Well, I guess the police know what they are doing better than you do, Mr. Madrid," said Bates. "Let me look in my file here, if the court will indulge me for a moment." Bates started leafing frantically through the large sheaf of papers in front of him. Madrid glanced down at me briefly, as if to say that no such report existed in the files. "It must be here," sputtered Bates. "It has to be here. The police . . ."

The judge waived the D.A. into silence and turned to Madrid. "You are raising the possibility that the body found at the covered bridge on campus is not Maxine March, but someone else?"

"I am saying just that. I am saying that the remains are that of an unknown white female and not Maxine March. Because the county has specified that my client killed Maxine March, he cannot be held in custody if there is any doubt that the person he is charged with killing may still be alive."

"Totally false! I cannot allow this charade to continue!" Bates was shouting now and gesturing toward the judge with both arms.

"Sit down, Mr. Bates. I will decide this matter, and I do not appreciate your choice of words here. Any trial or hearing over which I preside is not a charade. I will have to cite you if I hear one more outburst. Is that clear?"

"Yes, Your Honor. I apologize."

Madrid smiled ever so slightly as he continued. "I would not insult the intelligence of this court, Your Honor, by contending that my client deserved release if I thought there was a chance that he was a danger to the community. I simply do not want to see a miscarriage of justice."

Bates looked as if he might burst, but he remained quiet.

"I am sure you would not, Mr. Madrid, but you can save the long explanations as to your motive here today." The judge looked around the room and then at me before speaking. "The court is persuaded by the questions raised by Mr. Madrid that the state is not certain who was found dead. Certainly, there are no DNA samples to prove that the body found is that of Maxine March. That puts Mr. Martindale's involvement in the crime in question. I have no choice but to release him on his own recognizance, subject to rearrest and a further court appearance after the police and the district attorney's office have determined who is dead here." Judge Andrews banged her gavel once on the bench and quickly left the room.

I shook Madrid's hand. "How did you find that out?" I whispered into his ear as I hugged him.

"I didn't find anything out. In my business, you learn to throw a bunch of stuff at the wall and see what sticks. Bates is a careless attorney, and I guessed that he hadn't done his homework. I'll let them process you out, and we'll go have a cup of coffee."

❀ ❀ ❀ ❀ ❀

I walked out the door of the Benton County Correctional
Facility an hour later, temporarily, at least, a free man. Madrid
was leaning against a tree talking on his cell phone as I strolled
up to him.

"Okay, just find out all you can and let me know," he said,
then pushed the OFF button. "Nice to see you on the outside
again," he said, turning to me with a big smile on his face.

"Nice to be seen on the outside," I said, stepping into the sun.
"I don't think I could have stood being in there much longer."

"Come on, let's get out of here."

I followed him across the courthouse grounds to Monroe
Street, where he led me to a small red convertible.

"Habitual criminals never say a thing about being locked up,"
he said, as he opened both doors with his clicker, and we got in.
"Some of the guys I represent have been arrested so many times
that another trip to the slammer means nothing to them—no
shame, no embarrassment. Nothing. For people like you, the
humiliation is more than they can bear. Am I right?"

"Boy, you can say that again," I sighed. "I feel right now that I
will never, ever live this down. My career is ruined, and I may be
financially ruined too, all for something I did not do. I was
framed. But I guess that's what they all say, right?"

"Well, as a matter of fact, they do," he smiled, as he turned
right on Second Street and headed south. "But you, I believe."

We drove a few blocks, then turned onto a side street and
stopped at one of the oldest coffee places in town, The Beanery.
This was an institution in Corvallis, popular long before the
ubiquitous Starbucks opened its first store anywhere. It was far
enough away from campus that I was not likely to run into any
colleagues or friends.

He motioned for me to sit at a table in the corner and walked
over to order for us. He returned in a few minutes with two

coffees and a couple of cookies. "You're probably hungry, but this is all they've got. You can eat a hearty dinner later."

"Thanks," I said, devouring a cookie in just a few bites.

"Here, have mine," said Madrid. "You need it more than I do."

I quickly ate the other cookie.

"That call I made was to my investigator, a guy named Raymond Pearl. He's a retired cop from New York, and he's real good. Kind of rough around the edges, but he knows what he's doing."

"Great. I'm not sure how I'm going to pay for this, but right now, I don't care. I want to get this over with and get my name cleared." I drained the cup and walked over for a refill.

When I got back, Morales got down to business. "Okay, now tell me about Maxine March and your involvement with her. I'll want to get it in writing later for the file. But give me a short version right now."

"I met her about a year ago when she came into my office to sign up for a class. We liked one another right off and eventually became close friends."

"You're not going to tell me that you were hitting on a coed, Tom," he said, a serious look on his face.

"Never. It was nothing like that. She is—was—my age. I kept it strictly business at first. In fact, she kind of pursued me. She followed me to my house at the coast once, and I sent her away. But then I kind of fell for her—at least in my mind. I didn't let her know, at first."

"The police said you stalked her. Where did they get that?"

I blushed and took another drink of coffee. "I got jealous at one point and drove by her house a few times to see if she was there. She started getting real friendly with another student, Gary Hancock—the guy who tried to kill me."

"The guy who killed the two presidential candidates?"

"Yes, that's him. They had something in common in their opposition to the Vietnam War in the sixties. They were the same age and had the same grievances. Stuff they carried over from that time. Hancock, especially, could not get beyond it. It consumed his life and really caused his death."

"It sounds like it," said Madrid, looking up from the legal pad he was writing notes on.

"So they started hanging out together, and probably sleeping together, too. Maxine could be promiscuous. In some ways, that was part of her charm. She was so free with everything, whether it be her way of thinking or her . . ."

"Body?" guessed Madrid.

I nodded.

"Did the two of you? . . ."

"Sleep together?"

"Yeah, I hate to get so personal, but questions like this are bound to be asked by the prosecution."

"No, things had not gotten that far. I'm old-fashioned when it comes to sex. It takes me a long time to commit. I've never just tumbled into bed when I first meet a woman. Part of it is reserve and part of it is my position as a university professor. I consider myself a role model. That also added to my caution with Maxine. Even though she was only taking one course and was my age, our relationship bothered me. She was—at least technically—a student."

"But I guess you overcame your inhibitions eventually."

"Yeah, I did. I really liked her. I think I was falling for her in a way that had never happened to me before. But we took it very slowly. In fact, the last time I saw her was when I took her on a picnic about a week before she died. That was the first time we'd ever had a date."

"I guess no one is going to come forward later to tell the D.A. that they saw you checking into a motel in Albany? I'm sorry, but

I have to ask questions like that because the wrong answer can cause us serious problems later."

"I understand. No, that is the truth, and no one can say they saw anything like that because it did not happen."

Madrid nodded. "Good, I figured as much, but I had to ask."

I continued my story. "So, we went on the picnic, and as we were sitting there in McDonald Forest, we heard a loud explosion. I investigated and discovered the burning car and the body of Hector Morales, your old client, inside."

"The now headless Hector Morales," said Madrid, shaking his head, a sad look on his face. "He turned out to be a real bad guy. Like all migrants, though, he had a tough life."

"I'm sure he did and, whatever he was involved in, he did not deserve to die that kind of death." I shuddered at the memory of opening the car door and having Morales's head roll onto the ground toward me.

"Anyway, I called the police, and the head of campus security arrived with a team of her people."

"That would be Angela Pride."

"Yes."

"I understand that the two of you had a thing a while back."

"Yeah, we did. Several 'things' over the years I have known her. We broke up a couple of years ago, but we're still friends. At least, I thought we were. She treated me pretty badly on the day I was arrested. Tricked me and lied to me."

"I guess, in her mind, she was doing her job," he said. "But we can talk about all of that later, because it might aid us in your trial. The way police arrest a suspect can sometimes help a lot— I mean, if it is handled badly. If it is not handled by the book." Madrid jotted something down on a page, tore out the page, and put it in his pocket.

"I don't want to get her into any trouble."

"Look, Tom. Your life as a free man is at stake here. Don't go all mushy on me because you were once intimate with this woman. This is far too serious for that."

"I know, I know," I shook my head. "I seemed to have picked the wrong woman to fall for."

Madrid continued to take a lot of notes. "So, nothing happened between you and Maxine March, other than innocent flirtation? I mean, you didn't have sex."

"Like I said before, we did not. It may have been headed there, but it hadn't happened yet. We kissed out there in the forest at our little picnic and it was nice, but we did not roll on the ground and have passionate sex. I'm too straitlaced for that."

"I hate to keep pressing you on this, but it is a key point in your defense."

"I understand."

"Good. I take it that Ms. March was a little more passionate."

"Yeah, I guess she was. As I mentioned, she was all over me early on at my house. That still seems odd to me, given our chaste relationship later."

"Maybe she thought you'd like her better if she let you know that she was available," he said. "Maybe she really wanted to get into your class." Madrid smiled for the first time since we met the year before.

"That would be a first. I may be a popular teacher, but I do have my limits! And I am usually dealing with kids who are barely out of their teens. I never allow any kind of prurient thoughts of any kind about the young ladies I teach!" Now it was my turn to smile.

"I am sure parents all over the state are heartened by that statement," he said, still smiling.

He and I had been kidding up to this point, but this is something I had always taken very seriously. "It does happen, but not by me,"

I said. "It is such a betrayal of trust by a teacher to take advantage of kids who are put in your care when they are sent to college."

"I'm with you on that. Okay, now let's talk about Maxine's former husband, Duncan Delgado. Tell me what you know about him."

"I first met him on jury duty during your case."

"Hector Morales's case?"

"Yes. We chatted a bit before the selection process, and he said some pretty harsh things about Mexicans. Knowing he felt that way, I remember thinking that you were choosing a biased person to pass judgment on your client. I would not have had that bias."

"Of course, I didn't know that," he said.

"Of course, you didn't. It was just ironic, that's all. At any rate, it seemed like Morales knew who Delgado was. A look of recognition passed between them in the courtroom."

"And, of course we found out later that Delgado had signed his application for a green card," said Madrid. "I missed it, but there it was in the files, plain as day. What else happened?"

"You know about the use of the illegals by Delgado in his virus research?"

Madrid nodded and kept writing.

"I saw Morales out there at the lab the night the people were delivered. He and Delgado were arguing about something."

Madrid consulted some papers in a folder. "I have a state police report on that incident—they found no trace of anybody in the lab or the basement of the lab."

"It was like a dungeon. Really horrible with no toilet facilities and a dirt floor and sick monkeys in the other rooms. I was there. I know what I saw. Very bad!"

"So Delgado somehow got those people and the monkeys out of there between the time you saw him and when the SWAT team arrived the next morning?"

"I guess so. He is very smart and resourceful. Was he even questioned about this?"

"Only in a perfunctory way, from the look of it," he said, gesturing toward the papers in his hand. "So, what do you know about his research project?"

"It was on Ebola virus, the most deadly in the world. It breaks out in various African countries from time to time and is almost always fatal. People who get it bleed from every opening in their body. It is a horrible way to die, but the odd thing is that people who get it die so quickly that there is only time for them to infect those around them. As a result, the outbreaks usually last only a short time.

"There were a few cases in Germany where it is called the Marburg virus, after the town where the victims lived. The worry has always been that a terror group would somehow carry the virus to this country and infect thousands of people at once. It would be a catastrophe of immense proportions—on the scale of the 9/11 attacks in New York and Washington."

"God, yes. Maybe even worse," he said.

"Scientists have only scant evidence of its effects on people, however," I continued. "No one has ever had human subjects to test possible vaccines on because victims died so quickly. I guess Delgado decided he would be the first to try to develop a vaccine. He expected lots of kudos for doing that and maybe lots of research money. Never mind that the test subjects would probably die. The ethical considerations would prevent the very thing he was aiming to achieve. No reputable funding agency or scientific institution would touch him if he killed people to get his test results."

"Wouldn't he know that? Why would he risk his reputation to achieve such a tainted result?" asked Madrid.

"Because he's nuts," I said. "I don't mean slightly odd, I mean certifiably crazy."

"So you think that he killed Morales and Maxine because they knew too much about him?"

"That's precisely what I'm saying." I drank more coffee and got up to get another refill.

"And he framed you for her murder." Madrid did not make this statement in the form of a question, which gave me some hope.

"You are beginning to believe me?" I asked.

"I would not be here if I didn't," he said. "I've always got too many cases to take one I don't believe in. This case is important to both of us. I got blindsided by Delgado myself when I didn't notice on that immigration form that he knew Morales years ago. I need to get a little closure on this, too."

"Lucky for me," I laughed, shaking my head at the prospect of not having a good attorney like Madrid to help me. "Where is Delgado now? Is he still around town?"

"His office says he is on his way to a conference in Europe. His assistant even gave me his itinerary—without my asking for it."

"Like she was told to do that if anyone asked?"

"You think?" said Madrid, shaking his head. "You can bet he set this up, and it's clear to me that he framed you. Why, I am not sure. He is one smart hombre. First, I've got to prove that you had nothing to do with Maxine March's death. We need to get your name cleared so you can get on with your life. But to do that, I need to focus the blame on someone else."

"Like Duncan Delgado."

"You got it. And maybe if things heat up around here for him, he will panic and we'll find out what happened to Maxine March and those poor people you saw."

"Yeah, I think about them a lot," I said. "I still see the face of that one little boy who looked so bewildered and frightened."

"That bastard Delgado," said Madrid, banging his fist on the table. "He needs to pay for whatever he did to them. They're his own people, for God's sake!"

By this time, we had emptied our cups of coffee and I was drained of energy. I guess I looked it.

"Tom, you've got to get some rest. You look terrible."

"I feel terrible and look grungy." I took a quick whiff of my shirt. "And I smell bad, too!"

"Jail does that to you. First time you've seen the underbelly of life, I take it?"

"Yes, it is. I am used to viewing life from the sidelines, careful to stay out of the way while I take notes for a story. I prefer that distance."

Madrid smiled and extended his hand. "I'll work to make it so. Now let's get you home and into the shower."

June 23, 2005

ven though I had taken a shower the night before when I got home, I took another long one the next morning. The hot water felt good on my poor, beat-up body. I let it blast me for twenty minutes or so. Even then, I hated to get out. As I toweled off, I glanced at the clock on a table in the adjacent bedroom. It was nearly 11 A.M.—I had slept over twelve hours.

Although I didn't have to be anywhere special, I felt an urgency to get started on clearing my name. I dreaded the averted eyes, the pitiful glances, the suspicious looks, and I hated to think of the long explanations I'd need to make over something that was not my fault.

Before tackling any of this, I needed something to eat. After putting on jeans and a T-shirt, I walked into my small kitchen. I wasn't sure what, if anything, there was to eat. Then I remembered: I had gone shopping on the day before I was arrested. To my delight, I found orange juice, eggs, bread, and jam in the refrigerator. I made coffee and set about making an omelet.

Before I ate this delicious looking repast, I stepped outside to get the local newspaper. I scanned it as I started to eat. Unfortunately, the story of my release was not on page one, as the story of my arrest had been. Right there on the spot, I joined the ranks of disgruntled sources everywhere in decrying that media tendency.

LOCAL MAN RELEASED was the headline on a short news brief on page ten. It went on to note that I had been let out of jail on my own recognizance, but said nothing about any lack of evidence against me. *The Oregon University professor had been charged with the murder of one of his students last week.* And that was about it. My affiliation and name were there, but nothing about my declaring my innocence or Maxine's age. It sounded as though I had murdered an eighteen-year-old coed and might get away with it. I threw the paper on the floor in disgust at just about the same time the phone rang.

"Hello."

"Hi, Tom. It's Angela."

"Hello." I tried to keep the coldness out of my voice, but I felt only anger toward her as someone I had once considered a close friend. "Are you assembling a SWAT team to rearrest me?"

"That is not fair, Tom. I was only doing my job. I . . ."

"That's what the Nazis said, except they were 'only following orders.' You could have cut me some slack. You could have warned me. We were once close, Angela. I deserved better than that." Tears filled my eyes as I thought of the humiliation my arrest had brought upon me and on Maxine. Dead, gone. Never to be seen again.

"Tom, I felt I had no choice. You're the one who became involved with this March woman. You are the one . . ."

"Don't you dare say her name! You didn't know her. She was a fine person, and you make it sound like she was some kind of whore."

"I didn't know her, but you certainly did!"

"Stop this, Angela! Why are you calling me and harassing me? I'll call your chief or the president of the university and report this!" I was sobbing by this time—both in rage and in sorrow. I wiped my nose and my eyes. It was time for a counterattack. "You are sounding a bit jealous, Angela. Miss never-get-your-uniform-wrinkled Pride! You couldn't stand it that we couldn't get it on, but that I was happy with someone else. Admit it! You were jealous, so you arrested me on a trumped-up charge the minute you could! You're glad Maxine March is dead! But if you think that means I'll take you back, you are sadly mistaken."

A little exaggeration never hurts in the heat of battle.

"TAKE YOU BACK?" she shouted. "I NEVER TOOK YOU IN THE FIRST PLACE! You were never much of a lover, so what's to miss?!"

"It always comes back to that, doesn't it! My lovemaking skills! Things would have gone better if you weren't always such an ice cube. You wouldn't know true passion if it bit you in the ass. Maxine March had more passion in one little finger than you will ever have in your whole body! I'm hanging up now, Angela."

"I called to see if you needed anything, but it's pretty obvious that you are too busy feeding on your hatred for me and the rest of the world to care about much else!"

"Don't call me again!" I said. "If I see you, I will turn my head and cross the street or do anything else to get away from you. And I am putting you on notice that I will prove my innocence."

"Don't tell me. Mr. Private Detective is going back to work! Tom, the things you do always make it worse for the trained professionals who know how to solve crimes. Stay out of this, or

I swear I will have you arrested! Stay out of this, or I swear I will see that you lose your job!"

"YOU CAN GO TO HELL, ANGELA!" I shouted as I slammed the receiver down.

In my rage, I dropped my plate on the floor as I was clearing the table. I got on my knees to pick up the pieces, when the phone rang again.

"Did you think up another way to screw me?" I yelled into the phone.

"I guess we're not having a very good morning," said the voice at the other end of the line.

"Paul? God, I'm glad to hear from you!"

Paul Bickford is an Army Special Operations officer I had met several years ago on a research trip to the Arctic. He had reappeared in my life earlier this year when he handled the security operations for the appearance of the chairman of the Joint Chiefs of Staff as the University's Commencement speaker. He saved my life a few days before my arrest, and promptly disappeared. This is one of his most common characteristics. He handles things quietly, then drops out of sight.

"Where are you?"

"If I told you that, professor, I'd have to kill you." Bickford is a great kidder, or at least he thinks he is. "I can't get to Oregon just now, but I wanted to talk to you about your little problem."

"It's more than a little problem. It's gigantic!"

"For you, maybe, but not the rest of the world."

"Agreed. I always get a bit testy when I spend time in jail." Tossing these witty remarks back and forth made me feel better right away.

"You're out now, and you seem to have a good attorney. I checked out Lorenzo Madrid, and he's the real deal. He cares about something other than charging a high hourly rate. He will take good care of you on this."

"Wait a minute, Paul. How do you know about who my attorney is? Do you know Lorenzo? Wait, don't tell me. You aren't at liberty to tell me. I know your drill."

"You're learning, professor. Don't ask, and I won't have to refuse to tell. Let's just say that I keep tabs on my friends who are in trouble. And I also check out their attorneys to make sure they are up to the job."

"But, how? . . ."

"You will have to trust me on this, Tom. Hang on a sec . . ." Bickford put his hand over the mouthpiece so I could not hear what he was saying. I did hear the roar of a jet plane in the background.

"Paul, are you at an airport somewhere?"

"What?" said Bickford as he came back on the line.

"I asked if you were at an airport somewhere."

"Yes, I am, and I've got to get on a plane in a few minutes. I wanted to see if you had survived your incarceration and to tell you that I will help you all that I can to find out who killed Maxine March—or who everyone thinks is Maxine March."

"Lorenzo raised that question in court and that got me released. Did you put him up? . . ."

"I am not an attorney, Tom."

"I know that. But you still raised the point with him."

"He was working on that strategy when I contacted him."

"Do you have evidence that she is alive? What do you know?"

"Only suspicions, not hard evidence. I've got to get on this plane."

"Wait, Paul. Tell me more. You can't leave me hanging like this. I loved Maxine March. I need to know if she's dead!"

"That I cannot say for certain. All I know is that local authorities, including your old girlfriend, Lt. Pride, jumped to

their conclusions pretty hastily and assumed the dead woman
was your Maxine without doing any tests. You know the body
was burned up pretty badly."

I felt the urge to throw up. I had not known that Maxine had
burned to death.

"Your faculty card was there with blood on it, and you know
the rest. Lots of jumping to conclusions there, and you paid
dearly for it, Tom, you really did."

"So what can we do? How can we find out where she is, dead
or alive? And who was the woman they found, if it wasn't
Maxine? And where is Delgado?"

"As always, Tom, you have many more questions than I have
time to answer. I've got to go—and fast. I've been keeping some
colonels and a two-star waiting. I'll contact you as soon as I can.
In the meantime, get some rest and keep out of trouble. Can you
promise me that?"

"You know I can't do any of that, Paul." I was chuckling,
despite my grief and worry.

"Okay. Let me give you something to keep you going. Check
out an abandoned sanitarium over near the coast. Not sure
where it is."

"Sanitarium? On the water or in the mountains? I need more
to go on than that, Paul!"

There was no sound on the other end of the line. As always,
Paul Bickford was gone.

he only lucky thing that had happened to me in months was the fact that all of my personal troubles had coincided with summer vacation. And, for the first time in years, I was not scheduled to be working. Wisely, I had long ago decided that I would need the summer to recover from my management of the presidential search process. I had planned to divide my time between Corvallis and my house on the coast, reading and resting. I didn't know I would be spending the summer clearing my name and regaining my reputation. At this point, I wasn't sure if it would be possible to do either, but I had to try.

I started my search for the sanitarium Bickford had mentioned by doing a Google search on such facilities in Oregon. What I got was a series of listings for current spas and private psychiatric hospitals. All were located near major cities in the state, not the coast. Searching for "Oregon Sanitariums—Historic" yielded the name of a now abandoned one in eastern Oregon next to a hot springs. Because of its mineral-rich, 209-degree spring, it had thrived from 1908 to the 1950s as a treatment center for people with a number of ailments. A promotional pamphlet was quoted on its Web site: "A poultice from the sediments at the bottom of the lake relieves the most agonizing forms of rheumatism. . . . Fully ninety percent of all cases of rheumatism, neuralgia, and all nervous disorders, hemorrhage of the kidneys, and earlier stages of Bright's disease, all ordinary ulcers, sores and eczema in all its forms, can be cured by use of the water, or a combination of water and mud." The entry went on to say that the doctor who had founded the place also believed that the hot sulfuric baths killed the organism that caused syphilis.

As always, I had gotten carried away in my research. This material on the sanitarium was all very interesting, but it was not the place I was looking for. What could Bickford have been talking about? I trolled on, but found nothing.

I spent the rest of the day catching up on cleaning, laundry, and my mail—anything to get my mind off my troubles and Maxine. Late in the afternoon, I decided to drive to Newport and my house just south of the Yaquina Head Lighthouse. I always felt better over there. I was also hoping that the news of my arrest and subsequent release would not have made it across the Coast Range.

*   *   *   *   *

Before I drove to my house north of town, I decided to stop for lunch at a new seafood restaurant on the Bayfront, the oldest section of town. This welcome addition to the culinary offerings of the area served fish that had been caught in some of the boats that tied up across the street in the harbor, home of the largest fishing fleet in the state.

After I had finished some fish tacos and a glass of beer, I felt a lot better able to face the world. I paid my bill and decided to walk down the boardwalk that skirted the water, then turned onto the sidewalk that passed a combination of canneries, tourist attractions, gift shops, and galleries that ran for three blocks. It felt good to smell the fresh air, with the occasional whiff of fish. In the background, I could hear the barking of the enormous sea lions that had all but ruined several floating moorages below some of the shops.

At the end of the third block with the Coast Guard station up ahead on the hill, I crossed the street and began to look in windows of several art galleries before going back to where I had parked my car. My eyes darted quickly past the usual scenes of lighthouses, sea gulls, and crashing waves and stopped abruptly on a watercolor of a large building that looked abandoned and in disrepair.

A small bell tinkled as I opened the door and stepped into the gallery. I walked to the back and waited while the only person on duty finished talking to two women in sweatshirts.

"Do you have postcards and film?" the larger of the two asked.

"I'm sorry but we don't," said the clerk, a young woman with long blond hair tied into a ponytail. "You might try the gift shop next door."

"Well," huffed the other woman, "don't you like tourists? We keep places like this in business!"

The young woman kept smiling, albeit a bit more forced than before. "I think they can help you."

The two women stomped out, muttering all the way.

"When an American is an ugly American in her own country . . . ," I said. "You don't have to comment, but I could tell you get that all the time."

"People think we're a gift shop and don't seem to see that we're a gallery when they walk in the door," she said. "I don't want to be rude . . ."

"But it's very tempting," I added, unhelpfully.

"So, how may I help you?" she smiled.

"I was interested in that watercolor in the window of the old building. I wondered who painted it and where it was located."

She walked to the window and picked up the painting from its rack. I followed, grateful for the chance to see the work more closely. She handed it to me. I'm no expert on art, but the detail looked good to me. The ruined structure had a sad look, but at the same time, the artist had also managed to convey the spookiness that this place must evoke for anyone who saw it up close.

"Who's the artist?"

The young woman took the painting and turned it over. "We usually put only a serial number on the back. Let me get it, and I'll look in my master registry for a name and the contact information." She walked to the rear of the gallery and pulled a large binder from under the counter. "Let's see . . . the artist is Pat Thompson. She lives in Lincoln City. I can give you the price and some details of the work, if you were calling her about that. She calls the piece *Descent into Madness*." She jotted down the pertinent information and walked back to me.

Then I did what I always do when I'm playing a role to get what I want: I told a little white lie. These lies never hurt anyone, but do save time in the long run. "I wanted to talk to her about her technique. Very good brushstrokes and precise detail not usually seen in watercolors."

What bullshit! I didn't know a brushstroke from a spray can, but I hoped it sounded knowledgeable.

"Yes, I noticed that myself," she smiled. She put the painting back in the window, having decided on the spot that I would not be buying it.

I took the slip of paper containing the contact information. "Thanks a lot. You've been very helpful."

"Are you a beginner? I mean, are you just starting lessons?"

If she knew that I specialized in pictures with stick figures only, she would probably have thrown me out of the gallery.

"Not really. I am an amateur photographer, and I am trying to perfect a new technique that might look like watercolors but is really done with digital photography."

Additional bullshit, compounded by an outright lie. I had to get out of here.

"Oh, I love photography, too," she gushed. Looking around somewhat conspiratorially, she whispered, "I prefer it to oils and watercolors. So much more realism than a painter can possibly capture." Conspiracy over, she began speaking in a normal tone. "Take a card. The gallery owner loves displaying work by new artists using new techniques. I'll bet he'd show your stuff if you contacted him."

"When I'm ready, that would be great." Like in a hundred years.

I walked to the door and turned to wave as she began talking to another group of sweatshirt-clad women.

"Got any film?" asked one.

"How about T-shirts?" said the other.

n person, Pat Thompson looked just like she sounded on the telephone. She was a pleasant looking woman, probably in her seventies, with a nice smile and friendly eyes.

"Mr. Martindale, please come in," she said, as she stepped aside to allow me to enter. Her home was well furnished, but not ostentatious in the manner of some houses along the Oregon coast. As with many such homes, the view of the ocean overshadowed everything else. It was spectacular. To the west was the ocean itself, blue and shimmering in the summer sun. To the north was Cascade Head, a glorious, tree-covered headland.

"I've made some iced tea," she said, gesturing for me to sit down on a couch facing the windows.

"Sounds good to me," I said. "This is a great house. I wouldn't get anything done if I had this view."

"Do you live on the coast, Mr. Martindale?" she called from the kitchen.

"Tom. Please call me Tom."

"And I'm Pat."

"Actually, I do, in Newport, and I have a pretty good view, too—at least, out to sea. But you've got the Head to look at. It adds another dimension."

She walked back into the room carrying a tray containing a pitcher, two glasses, and a plate of cookies. "Yes, it inspires me when I paint. Lemon? Sugar?"

"Lemon only, please," I replied, squeezing a slice into one glass as I poured tea into both containers. I grabbed a cookie and took a bite.

"You're interested in *Descent into Madness?*"

"I was very taken by the title of your work. Very appropriate, given that spooky-looking building. I am interested in the watercolor, but not to buy it. I'm sorry if I gave you the impression that I was a potential customer. I'm wondering where that building is located. I'd like to go there to see it."

"Oh, I see." Pat did not look disappointed, only curious about my purpose. "I guess I'm wondering why you'd want to go to such a remote place," she said. "Are you a painter?"

"No, not at all. I sometimes take photos of old and abandoned buildings. That one struck me as a perfect candidate." I had slipped back into my lying mode, and I didn't like to be doing that. But how to tell her the truth without going into a lot of detail?

"Oh, yes, I see what you mean." She sipped her tea without saying anything more, but she didn't seem to believe me. I contemplated Cascade Head one more time and ate another cookie.

"Why don't you tell me what you want from me, Tom," she said. "It would be so much easier than all this beating around the bush."

"You're very perceptive, Pat."

"You don't get to be my age without learning how to read people."

Reluctantly, I would have to tell her at least part of my story, or I wouldn't get the information I had come to get. "Where to begin?" I gave her a brief synopsis about my need to find a friend who had vanished. I left out the part about my arrest for Maxine's murder and my release from jail. I hoped she had not read the Corvallis paper or seen the small item about me in *The Oregonian*. Thankfully, none of the Portland television stations had covered my arraignment. I told her that a person I trusted had hinted that my friend might have been held against her will in a place that sounded a lot like the building in her painting. Because the police were showing little interest in finding her, I said I wanted to go to the building to see if she had been there or, hopefully, was still there.

Pat considered all of this for a moment before speaking. "So someone is holding your friend against her will?"

"I have reason to think so."

"And who is this person?"

"Her ex-husband."

"Is this some kind of lover's quarrel—I mean, a triangle between the three of you?"

"Nothing like that."

This woman was proving to be very perceptive, but also a pain in the butt. Why wouldn't she tell me what I wanted to know so I could get out of here and find the sanitarium?

"Maxine March—that's my friend's name—and I are just good friends. I know her husband from where I work. But that . . ."

"And where is that?"

"I teach journalism at Oregon University." At least I hoped I still did. The jury was still out on that.

"And this man—the husband—teaches there, too?"

Why was she continuing to pepper me with all these questions? This was really annoying.

"Yes, he's a biologist."

"And the wife?"

"Ex-wife."

"Ex-wife, yes. What does she do?"

"She was a student of mine."

"Oh, so she's young?"

I could see where this was going—me getting cozy with a coed. And a married coed, at that.

"No, she is my age."

"Oh, yes, I see." Pat drank more tea and ate a cookie.

"Pat, I have to tell you that I don't see what any of this has to do with your telling me where this place is. If you'll do that, I'll get out of here and let you get on with your day."

"And tend to my knitting." She was smiling, but I could see that she was not about to let me intimidate her.

"I just meant that I don't want to take up so much of your time."

"You aren't being very forthcoming with me, Tom. I have all the time in the world to hear about this. It is very interesting."

You've got all the time to be nosy and find out things you really don't need to know, I thought.

"There's not much more to tell. I want to go there and have a look around. If I find out anything, I'll go to the police. They don't seem to be very interested in following up on Maxine's disappearance, as I've said. That is pretty much it in a nutshell." I folded my arms as if to say that I would not be answering any more questions.

She smiled and nodded. I think she got the message. "Well, okay. I think I have all the background I need for now."

For now! Good grief!

"The building is an abandoned hospital, part psychiatric, part therapeutic. There's some kind of hot springs on the property and that is what attracted the founders to the spot. It was a branch of a similar facility in eastern Oregon. The isolated location gave them the idea to add the psychiatric part."

"When was this?"

"Starting in the 1920s and continuing into the 1950s. It was abandoned after that because of the high cost of maintaining it in such a remote spot. And I think the state started building more facilities so there was less need for a private one like that."

Finally, we were getting somewhere.

"So, where is it, and how did you find it?"

"It is near the site of that old timber company town near Valsetz, in the Coast Range west of Monmouth. It was torn down in the 1970s, I think."

"Yes, I've heard of it. One of my former students did a photo essay on the town's last days for the newspaper where he was working. Not much there now, I gather."

"Nothing at all," she continued. "I went on an extended hike with a nature group I belong to—last fall, I think it was. I'm always looking for things to paint, so I was disappointed when all the buildings in the town were gone. But I kind of wandered off from the group at one point and climbed up on a ridge. As I looked across toward the west, I was surprised to see this large old building on the next ridge. When I looked at it through my binoculars, it seemed ideal for me."

"So, I suppose you walked there to see it at close range?"

"I wanted to do just that, but there was no way I could, as far as I could tell. We were out of time, and it looked like too long a hike for an old lady like me. So I did the next best thing: I used my new digital camera with the telephoto lens and took lots of shots of it. The detail turned out to be pretty remarkable, given the distance."

"Your watercolor is based on photos taken from far away? That is remarkable. Could I see the photos?"

"Yes, I have them right here," she said, handing them to me.

"Could I borrow one, for reference?"

"Of course. Help yourself. In fact, you can keep it. They are mostly the same shot anyway."

I pondered my next move with Pat Thompson. While I was grateful for her help, I did not want to involve her in this. For one thing, she might be in danger. If Duncan Delgado was holding Maxine at this place, I wasn't sure what he would do if they were discovered. Also, she was old and, even though she seemed in good health, I didn't want to take the responsibility if something happened to her. Let's face it, there was another reason: I didn't want an inquisitive lady who looked like Miss Marple butting in.

"Wow, is that the time?" I took an exaggerated look at my watch. "I have really taken up too much of your time already. How can I thank you—for the information and the tea and cookies." I stood up to leave and shook her hand.

"My pleasure," she said. "It's been fun for me, too. I hope I have been helpful and that you find your friend."

"Me, too. I hope it has all been a big misunderstanding." I walked toward the door.

"Oh, I almost forgot," she smiled, handing me a folder. "I should have you autograph these clippings from the Corvallis paper about your arrest and release. You're kind of a celebrity."

*   *   *   *   *

June 24, 2005

Early the next morning, I left my house for the drive to Valsetz. I hadn't responded to Pat's parting comment, only smiled and left hurriedly. I did not want to give her any more information than she already possessed. I had been upfront about what I wanted and treated her in a polite way from the moment I met her. I was not rude. If she sensed my rush to get away from her, she did not act like it. By the time I left, she knew almost everything that had happened to me. She was no dummy and could easily figure out why I would want to find this abandoned building. Although she was a nice lady, I hoped not to see her again.

I decided that the way to get to the sanitarium was to drive inland on Highway 18 and then take Highway 99W to Monmouth, then west to Falls City, the gateway to the Coast Range and the site of what was once Valsetz. Once there, however, the going would be tougher because the road was gravel only.

As soon as I drove onto the unpaved road, a swirl of dust enveloped my car. I was glad for air conditioning to keep the grime from getting all over the inside of my car and me. The roadway started to get steep about a mile in, but my car climbed easily around each switchback turn. I hoped that the fully loaded log trucks sometimes encountered on these back roads had gone the way of the town itself—I did not relish the thought of having to back down the very narrow road, which had no guard rails.

After another dusty hour, I drove into what once was the main street of Valsetz, although the timber company that had operated the small town had removed all traces of it. All the buildings had been torn down and the debris taken away. Indeed, only the concrete foundations remained of what I assumed were the company offices and store. Back from the road on side streets were the remnants of houses. Roof beams, wood planks, and parts of walls littered the ground.

In the school yard at the end of town, part of the fence and a dilapidated swing remained, the latter moving gently in the breeze. It was all very sad. If I felt bad about it, I could well imagine how difficult it had been for the people who lived and worked here.

I did not get out of my car, but drove to the end of town where the pavement ended and a barrier blocked my way. I turned off the engine, got out, and locked my car. Stepping around the barricade Pat had described to me, I could see the start of a path heading west through the brush. I glanced at my watch—it was just after noon. I would have plenty of time to locate the hospital and climb up the ridge to it.

I walked through the dense underbrush as quickly as I could. At various places, the thick cover of blackberries bushes and salal seemed to reach out and grab my pants legs. High above me, the limbs of the tall trees barely moved. It was beautiful and quiet, a pleasant respite from the craziness I had been through the past few weeks. I longed for some time to straighten out my life. It had become way too messy.

As I pressed on, the thought occurred to me more than once that I was very alone here. If anything happened, I would be unable to get help. I stopped and checked my cell phone. "No service," it blinked back.

After another fifteen minutes, I walked out of the brush and onto a promontory. As Pat Thompson had mentioned, the abandoned hospital was visible across a deep valley. I barely paused to look further. Without binoculars, I needed to be closer to see any details. I needed to be there to walk inside its dilapidated walls.

The path continued on the left and I walked along it, hoping that it would not run out. Fortunately, the brush was more sparse as the path continued downward, so I was able to make better time. I got to the floor of the valley in twenty minutes and found myself in a clear-cut area. The timber company had cut all the trees here and removed the logs. In their place was a mud-covered space with only a few stumps as a reminder of the forest that had once grown here. Now, it was not the brush that tried to entangle my legs, but the mud that tried to engulf my shoes. After the first step, my walking sneakers were totally black from the muck, as were my white socks. At one point, I had to reach down and pull one shoe back on after stepping in a particularly gooey spot.

I walked across this no man's land as fast as I could to the other side where the needle-covered ground resumed. Unfortunately, there was no path leading upward to the building. I walked left, but found no way through the underbrush; then I walked right.

The sound of running water kept me heading in that direction. As I rounded a bend in the cliff, I saw a waterfall flowing into a stream headed in the opposite direction. The sound and sight of the water bouncing off the rocks was a nice change from the mess I had just walked through. Seeing the water reminded me that I was thirsty, and I took a couple of swigs from the bottle of water I had brought with me. As I wiped my mouth on my sleeve, I noticed a spot on the other side of the stream where a path began.

I started to make my way to it by hopping on stones, but my foot slipped off the second rock and plunged into the water. I fell hard on my side, landing with a splash. Luckily, I did not sprain anything, but I was drenched to the skin—pants, shirt, both shoes. At least the mud was washed off my shoes.

I got to my feet and waited while the water drained off, then carefully stepped over to the bank and up onto dry land. I sat down and tried to ring out my pant legs by running my hands down over them. I removed my shirt and T-shirt and rung them out, shivering a bit at the coldness of the air. Even though it was a sunny summer day, the rays of sunlight had not penetrated the trees to reach me. After a while, I put my T-shirt back on and tied the sleeves of my shirt around my waist, hoping it would dry.

As I started to walk away, I felt water sloshing in my shoes. I sat down and took them off, then poured the water out. Next I took off and wrung out my socks. At least they and the shoes were now a bit cleaner. Finally, I was ready to leave, wrung out as best I could and hoping not to catch a cold.

The path was not overgrown, and I could walk up it easily. It was steep, however, and I was out of breath in a short time. I stopped to rest and looked out across the clear-cut area to the other side. As I did so, I caught a glimpse of sunlight reflecting on something shiny. Binoculars? Eyeglasses? With no way of knowing who might be looking at me, I resumed my climb.

In another ten minutes, I reached the top. More brush and trees awaited me, as did a path. Calculating the direction I had gone out of my way to the waterfall, I walked south in order to locate the building. It did not take me long to find it.

The building was even larger up close than it looked from afar. Its brick walls seemed out of place amid all the wood surfaces of the trees surrounding it. The broken windows gave it a sadness that reflected its abandonment and what had probably gone on inside.

As I walked closer, a flock of birds took flight from the eaves at one corner, startling me and causing me to jump. I walked on, soon encountering a wire fence that led to a locked gate. The lock was superfluous, however, because the fence post nearest the gate had fallen down, allowing easy entry. I stepped around the would-be barrier and ignored the faded sign:

NO TRESPASSING!
VIOLATORS WILL BE PROSECUTED!
OCEAN SPRINGS SANITARIUM

ven though many of the windows of the sanitarium were broken, they were just high enough off the ground to impede easy access. The main entrance looked quite grand with its double oak doors and stained-glass panels on either side. The only problem was that the steps had been sheered away from the building by a huge tree that had fallen across it and was still there. I walked along the front perimeter of the building and turned to go along the side, but found no door or any other way in.

The forest was trying to take possession of this structure. Limbs from the tall trees growing next to it extended over the roof and seemed, in spots, to be encroaching into breaks in the outer wall and the windows. The thick brush made it hard to move along and my foot caught at various points along the way. Twice, I almost fell. I stumbled on and eventually made it around to the back. Here, the encroachment of the forest was stopped by a wide expanse of gravel and several outbuildings to the left. Ahead, at dead center in the wall, was a door, partly obscured by vines.

I started tearing at the vines, which did not easily release their grip from the door. After a few minutes, I was able to find the doorknob. Although it was secured by a padlock, the hasp holding it in place was so rusty that it easily came loose. I pushed hard on the door, and it gave way. The force of my shove sent me barreling into the room so fast that I landed on my knees.

As I got to my feet, I realized that I was in the kitchen. Because natural light was limited by the small windows, I switched on my flashlight. As its beam skittered around, it picked out the objects you would expect to find: two large stoves, ancient refrigerators, cabinets for pans and dishes, a large work space in the center, and several large sinks.

I opened one cupboard and the light shown on bags of sugar, flour, salt, pepper, and a can of coffee. Many of the bags were torn, and a portion of their contents spilled out onto the shelves. Nearby, another cupboard with glass doors held dishes, stacked as if ready for use for the next meal. Drawers below held flatware and utensils.

I picked up a heavy pottery plate of the type found in restaurants in the 1930s. When I brushed the dust away, I saw that there was a small logo painted squarely in the center: "Ocean Springs Sanitarium" with a small wave surrounding it.

I walked through an open door to the next room—the dining room was larger than the kitchen and filled with large oak tables and matching chairs, most of them overturned, some of them broken, their legs and backs gone. The pieces that remained intact were in remarkably good condition. Any resourceful antique dealer would kill to possess even one of them. Large sideboards stood at the center of the four walls; each was topped with a mirror and its drawers held tablecloths and napkins.

Outside the main door to this room was the lobby. As I stepped into it, I looked up to the two-story ceiling and was surprised to see a stained-glass panel at the top. Remarkably, it looked to be in pristine condition with no broken panels.

To my left was a large counter of the type found in hotels. There was a work area beyond it for the admittance staff, and the rooms behind that were probably offices. The main part of the lobby contained a number of leather sofas, their straw stuffing spilling out from spots where the fabric had torn. Large oak library tables and wooden chairs also stood with the sofas. Most of the furniture had been pushed together in the center, with some pieces overturned.

To the left of the admitting area was a grand staircase. I glanced up to see beautifully carved banisters flanking the steps on both sides. I was not ready to go upstairs yet, however. I wanted to explore the long hall that I could see through the door to the south.

From force of habit, I tried the light switch just inside the entrance. It was one of those old models where you pushed a button—"on" at the top, "off" at the bottom—that clicked as you did so. No light glowed from above. As I expected, there was no power in the building.

Shafts of light penetrated the dimness at points along the hall where doors were open. Bright rays of sun shown through the window at the other end, as well. These were patient rooms; each had a bed with a white iron frame, a dresser, two white wooden chairs, and an armoire. As with the dining room furniture, the placement of the items in each room was haphazard. Some were in order, as if a person was living in them; others were in total disarray.

At first glance, the rooms did not look all that different from those I imagined in the resort hotels of the time. Closer scrutiny revealed bars on the tall windows. In one room, I picked up an old postcard dated 1924.

Ida May—I hope you are feeling better now after your last spell. I hope you know that we love you.

But we can't have you here with us right now. It is just not safe for your baby brother to have you home. It would be terrible if you would ever try to stab him again. Please know that you will always be our daughter.

Your loving, Papa

On the part with the address, someone—presumably Ida May—had written ALL LIES! The scene of Mount Hood on the reverse side had been defaced with a large X from corner to corner. I placed the postcard where I had found it, in the imprint it had made in the dust on the floor.

I walked to the end of the hall. Here, the room to the left was a nurse's station with a counter across the doorway and cabinets for medicines and desks for staff members filling the rest of the space.

The rooms on the other side of the hall were identical to those I had just seen, so I did not go into them. Feeling both sad and apprehensive at what I had seen, I felt the need to get back to the brighter light in the lobby. As I neared the door, a large rat ran across in front of me, probably heading for the kitchen and its remaining store of food.

It was now 3 P.M., and I wanted to look through the rest of the building and get out of here. Even though there were many hours of daylight left, I didn't want to risk having to walk back to my car in the dark, knowing that it would reach the ground more quickly because of the dense cover of trees up above.

As I started up the stairs, I stuck to the middle, carefully avoiding the handrails. Even the unbroken ones looked unsteady. At the top, I headed down the hallway in the same direction that I had traversed on the first floor. Here, a similar row of patient rooms lined both sides. At the end of the hall, however, I could see steam wafting up from below. Before I could examine it more closely, I heard a sound from the floor above me: one or two creaks as if someone was walking.

I retraced my steps to the stairway and ascended to the third floor hallway. A glance to the right revealed another long and dark hall lined with patient rooms. I turned to the left and immediately noticed a change in the configuration. In this section, the rooms looked more like hospital rooms—they were smaller and each held several beds. They also had the faint odor of disinfectant, human sweat, and urine.

Halfway down, the hall ended in a wall of frosted glass, with a single door at the center. It opened with a squeak, its hinges probably having gone without oil for nearly a century, and I stepped into another hall that ran only to the right. I walked along it and climbed some stairs. Through another door, and I was in a room that overlooked a large surgical suite. The equipment looked as old as everything else—tables, gurneys, trays to hold instruments—it all belonged in a medical museum. I walked to the end of the viewing room and down another stairway to the operating room floor. My entrance disturbed some bats, which flew around for a time and then exited through one of the broken windows.

This room was higher than the others on this floor, something I had not noticed from outside the building. Large windows on two sides allowed natural light to cascade into the room. This source would enhance the primitive lighting system above the operating tables.

Up close, the room was less pristine. The equipment was covered with dust, as were the various surgical instruments. Here and there, spots of blood marred the floor and the tiled walls.

As I walked to a door at the end of the operating room, I saw a shadow on the other side of the frosted glass.

"Hey," I called out, a mixture of fear and curiosity in my voice.
No reply, but the shadow stopped.

"Who is it?"

Nothing.

I ran back up the stairs to the viewing area and down the other
stairs and out into the hallway. Just as I got there, I saw a small
figure run down the hall to the main stairway. I followed in a fast
walk, not necessarily wanting to overtake this person too quickly,
but inquisitive nonetheless.

On the floor below, the figure was nowhere to be seen at first.
I looked both left and right to no avail. Then I heard a cough to
my right, as if the person deliberately wanted me to follow.

"*Andale, señor,*" said a voice.

The figure darted across the hall. Either a small man or a
woman, I calculated. Figuring I could defend myself in any
altercation between us, I took off in pursuit.

In my haste to follow the figure, I dropped my flashlight. As a
result, I did not see the large hole in the floor. Before I knew what
was happening, I plunged through it into the steam rising up
from below.

n the few seconds I had to contemplate my fate, I also worried about being burned to a crisp and breaking every bone in my body. I closed my eyes and braced for a bone-breaking landing. But it did not happen. In reality, I fell not into a bottomless pit with a boiling cauldron at the bottom, but onto something soft. In the dark, however, I could not tell exactly where I was.

Before I could get my bearings, I started to slide downward. This time, I wound up in a sitting position on a brick floor. I got to my feet and staggered toward a tiny pinpoint of light a few feet away. I pushed open a door and looked back. I had landed on a pile of mattresses that someone had stacked under the hole I had fallen through. Although the small room must have been used for storage, it had now been turned into a child's playroom.

As I stepped through the doorway, the steam that had lured me here poured into the opening. Natural light from windows high on the walls flooded the large space where I was standing.

I was in a rotunda, with a large pool in the center. Steaming water bubbled up from the middle of the pool; the rotten egg smell meant that it had a high sulfur content. It was these waters that lured developers into building the sanitarium eighty years before. Its unstoppable force meant it would go on forever, even if the building fell down around it—something it just might do very soon.

The water looked inviting, given the stiffness I could feel building up in my joints and legs. The long hike in and the fall had taken their toll on my aging body. But I had no time for anything like a restorative bath. I had to figure out who had lured me here. Was the tiny person trying to kill me or just get away from me?

I walked to an open door at the other end of the room and stepped into a large chamber containing a row of tubs and a row of hospital beds. Slings made of the same heavy material used in straitjackets dangled from the ceiling. A faded sign on the wall answered my unspoken questions.

TREATMENT PROTOCOL
Ocean Springs Sanitarium
For treatment of Arthritis,
Tuberculosis, Alcoholism,
Venereal Disease (Especially Syphilis)

1. *Submerge patient in sulfur bath (208 degrees F)*
2. *Leave in water until patient gets uncomfortable*
   —or for syphilis—convulses
3. *Move patient to bed area*
4. *Return patient to room when he regains*
   consciousness

Good grief! How could anyone survive such a treatment? I shuddered to think of the strain on these patients. I wondered what the success-to-failure rate had been. And the fatalities? If there was an Ocean Springs Cemetery, it had to be full of graves.

Beyond the person who lured me into my fall, I had not seen anything suspicious during the time I had been here. What had Paul Bickford been alluding to? What did this spooky place have to do with Maxine March's murder and my false arrest?

Stepping outside, I found myself at the opposite end of the building from where I had walked earlier. The single-story structure had been added onto the main building so that it enclosed the hot springs. There had been gardens here, no doubt to ease the troubled minds of those who had just been scalded in the tubs inside. Now, weeds had overwhelmed what appeared to have once been a carefully designed and well-maintained area.

A faint sound caused me to look up to a window on the third floor. A curtain fluttered, but I saw no one. I noticed that none of the glass in these windows had been broken.

I ran around to the back door and retraced my steps through the kitchen and dining room and back up the stairs. I kept climbing until I reached the third floor. Then I turned to the right and walked into an area I had ignored before because I thought it was empty.

As my eyes adjusted to the dim light, I thought at first that this section was no different from those on the other floors. Then, I noticed a closed door that looked less flimsy than the others. I walked to it and tried to open it. It did not budge. I heard something on the inside.

"Hello. Is someone there? I won't hurt you."

If you won't hurt me, I thought.

"I just want to talk."

Silence.

"Okay. I guess there isn't anyone there after all."

I carried on this exaggerated conversation with myself for a bit longer.

"I guess I will leave now."

I ceased this imbecilic line of chatter and pretended to walk away. I crept back to a point at the side of the doorway. I held my breath and waited.

In a minute or so, the door opened slightly. Soon, a head appeared and then shoulders and then a whole body.

"Looking for me?" I said, grabbing an arm and placing my foot between the door and the door casing so it could not be slammed shut.

"*Dios mio!*" A tiny woman faced me with a terrified look in her eyes.

"Don't worry. I mean no harm to you," I said. "I just want to talk." I released my grip on her arm and gestured for her to walk into the room behind. She did so quickly, and I followed.

The room was comfortably furnished with a sofa, tables, chairs, and two beds. The kitchen area contained a sink with a single water faucet and a small wood-burning stove. Everything was spotless.

I extended my arms out toward the woman with my hands pointing downward in a calming gesture. "I mean you no harm," I said. "Please do not be afraid of me. Do you speak English?"

She looked relieved and smiled. At this point, I heard a rustling sound in the corner and looked there. A small boy stepped out from what was probably the bathroom. His mother extended her arms to him, and he ran to her. The boy looked vaguely familiar.

I walked to him and bent down. "I am Thomas," I said, extending my hand.

The boy looked at his mother for reassurance. She nodded.

"Ronaldito." He shook my hand tentatively as if he had never done that before. We pumped our arms up and down in an exaggerated way, and he soon started giggling at this strange sensation. I laughed too, and that broke the tension.

"*Señor Tomas, por favor,*" the woman said, pointing to the sofa. I sat down.

"Maria Montez." Now it was our turn to shake hands. She sat opposite me in one of the chairs. "Yes, I speak English. You startled us. We are not used to many visitors lately. I am sorry if Ronaldito frightened you before, and that you fell through the floor—I was worried that you had hurt yourself badly. He was just playing. I rarely let him out of my sight, but he sometimes goes off on his own. Like any small boy, he is curious and that curiosity sometimes gets him into trouble."

We both looked at the boy who was standing next to her. He hung his head.

"I did not hurt myself. I am okay." I smiled at him and raised both arms and flexed my muscles. They both laughed. "I was walking in the forest and discovered this place." I began with some small talk, because I didn't intend to tell Maria and Ronaldito my real reason for being here. "I was surprised to find such a large place in the forest, and just couldn't stop exploring it."

Ronaldito looked at the floor.

"It's okay. Remember, I am okay." I smiled, and he relaxed again. "So, how do you happen to be living out here?

"It is, as you say, a long story," said Maria. "I came from Mexico with Ronaldito last year with a group of others from my village. We paid a *coyote* $1,000 each to get us across the border. That was in California. Then we were put in touch with a man who worked for Señor Delgado."

Bingo! The pieces of the puzzle were starting to fall into place. I tried to conceal my excitement at what she was telling me.

"We were driven up to Oregon by this man and moved into a tiny room under some kind of laboratory. It smelled bad, and there were monkeys in cages in the other rooms."

At the word "monkey," Ronaldito's eyes grew big as he remembered the place.

"Why did Señor Delgado take you to that place? Did he tell you?"

"Not exactly. The *coyote* mentioned that we would be involved in a medical experiment. I did not like the sound of that, but I liked the idea of earning money for it so I could pay back the *coyote*.

"You were paid money for what you did?"

"Yes, five dollars a day. Plus food and a place to sleep."

"So, what did you have to do?"

"I never found out. The night we arrived, Señor Delgado woke us up, and we left that place in a hurry. He said the *la migra* was coming, and we might be caught and sent back to Mexico."

There were other people with her in that room. I had seen them.

"Were you the only ones there?"

"Oh, no. There were maybe ten others."

"Where are they? Do they stay here?" I gestured around the room with my hand.

"No, *señor*, we are the only ones here. I am not sure where the others have gone. Señor Delgado drove us here himself. I guess the others were put in different places."

"Does Señor Delgado come here to visit you?"

"No, but he sends someone to bring us food and make sure we are feeling good."

I shuddered to think of what Delgado was planning for Maria and Ronaldito, but he was keeping them safe for some reason. Possible future experiments. He didn't do anything without an ulterior motive.

"Why don't you let me take you back to Corvallis. I can put you in touch with some social agencies or churches to help you get started.

A look of horror crossed her pretty face. "No, no, no, *señor*. I fear that *la migra* will come and send us back to Mexico and even take Ronaldito away from me." She pulled the boy close to her as she spoke.

It would do no good for me to try to explain the danger she might be in from Delgado—that could possibly be far worse than anything the immigration service would do. But she would not believe me, so I kept quiet for now.

"But you can't live here forever. Ronaldito needs to go to school. You need to get a job. You need to live a normal life."

She smiled faintly. "*Señor Tomas*, this is the most normal my life has been since my husband was killed two years ago. This all seems nice to me—as you say, 'normal'."

And you don't need a do-gooder like me to interfere, I thought.

"I see what you are saying," I said, deciding I would try to help them as soon as I could. "I will not tell anyone you are here. But I will look in on you from time to time to see if you need anything."

"*Gracias, señor.*"

"When did you see Señor Delgado last?"

Maria thought for a moment and said something to Ronaldito in Spanish. "It was about two weeks ago. The day he came to see the other lady."

My heart jumped into my throat. "Other lady?"

"Yes, I never did talk to her, but I saw her with him by his car. From the window, I saw the two of them."

Maxine was alive! I knew it! I tried to keep my excitement in check.

"Was he taking her in or out?"

"Out, I think. I had heard someone walking on the floor below for a day or two after we came here. I was too frightened to go there to see for myself, and I would not let my son go there, either. I would say to him, *'diablo'* and that was enough." She turned to Ronaldito. "You did not see the señora, did you, *mi hijo?*"

"No, *mama.*"

I could tell from the scared look on the little boy's face that her threat had worked. He had not gone anywhere near those sounds.

"Thank you so much for talking to me, Maria. I will keep my word, but I want you to promise to leave here if you feel you are in danger. Get to a phone and call 9-1-1 or even me if that happens. Here is my number. I can try to get help to you and see that you find another place to live." I handed her my card, doubting that she would call, or even be able to find a telephone if she wanted to. In all truth, what I suggested was impossible, but I had to say something.

"We have gotten very good at hiding, *señor.* You can count on that."

"I will leave now. I am going to look around a bit before I leave, so do not be afraid if you hear me walking around. Okay?"

They both nodded.

I walked to the door and stepped out into the hall. *"Adios, mi amigos."*

They waved as I walked down the hall. As soon as Maria closed the door, I raced to the stairs and down to the second floor, my heart racing. Maxine was gone from here, but maybe I could find something she had left behind. The hall was dark in the fading afternoon light—a reminder that I would need to leave soon if I did not want to spend the night in the sanitarium. This was a part of the building I had not explored before. My fall and the meeting with Maria and her son had distracted me.

Halfway down the hall, I came to a steel door with a small window at eye level. I could barely decipher the faded lettering on the sign:

PSYCHIATRIC WARD
NO ENTRANCE WITHOUT
PROPER AUTHORIZATION

I tried the door, although I expected it to be locked. It would not budge when I put my shoulder up against it and pushed. Then I took a more determined approached and pulled back before I pushed. Nothing moved. I examined the door and the door frame more closely and realized that both were made of reinforced steel—and they looked new. Delgado had gone to great pains to secure this section of the sanitarium, and it would be impossible for me to get in without using a crowbar or dynamite.

"HELLO. HELLO. ANYBODY THERE?" I put my ear to the door and waited for even a muffled sound from the other side. Silence. I walked over to the other side of the hall and sat down on a long wooden bench to think.

Delgado had brought Maxine here weeks ago, I presume under duress. Maybe he had drugged her. Why else would she stay? She truly seemed to hate him.

I was certain now that he had faked her death and framed me for killing her. With me out of the way in jail and Maxine under his control, no one would be able to prove anything against him. The Mexicans he had brought into the country illegally to use in the experiments were hidden in places unknown, except for Maria and Ronaldito.

"MAYBE HE'S UP THERE!"

A voice from below broke my train of thought. Then I heard dogs barking.

From my vantage point, I could see four men in sheriff's uniforms running toward the building. Straining on their leashes and pulling them with every ounce of strength in their bodies were four Doberman pinschers.

ran toward the west end of the building, away from where I expected them to enter through the same kitchen door I had used. As far as I knew, that was the only way to get in.

I quickly reached the end room and went in. The furniture was covered with dust, and I had to beat back thick cobwebs as I hurried to the window. I didn't expect to see the guards because I could hear them—and their snarling dogs—running around to the back of the building. The fact that the window had no glass in it made it easy for me to step out onto a small ledge that ran around the entire structure. It was faced with wire mesh, I suppose to keep inmates from jumping off.

Looking down, I could see a small porch that adjoined the rooms where Maria and her son were living. I grabbed the top of the mesh and swung my body around until I was hanging halfway down. From this point, I calculated that I would not break my ankles when I let go. I was right. I landed without so much as a twinge.

Maria and Ronaldito were looking out at me from the window. I put a finger to my lips and kept moving, away from the loud noises I could hear as the men came crashing into the lower floor. The dogs were howling in their frenzy to get to me.

At this end of the building, the ground was higher because a hill had been hollowed out to accommodate the hot springs into the design of the room below. It was not all that much of a leap from where I was to the hill. The steam wafting out of the windows helped hide me from view, as did the dwindling daylight. I landed and immediately crouched down behind some tree stumps. When it seemed safe, I ran toward the forest.

I did not look back or contemplate the fates of Maria and her son. I assumed they would hide from the men and their dogs as they had from me. And the deputies might not look around the building all that closely. After all, I was their main quarry.

I skirted the building by sticking to the forest and then retraced my steps back down the cliff and across the clear-cut area. I did not run, but kept up a fairly brisk pace.

At one point, I stopped abruptly when I heard a sound behind me. I held my breath and waited behind a tree, my heart pounding. I peeked out in time to see a deer walk to a nearby bramble of blackberries and begin to eat. She barely looked up as I came out of my hiding place and turned in the opposite direction.

I reached the parking area and my car in about an hour. As a precaution, I stayed out of sight. Even though it was dark, I did not want to take the chance that one of the deputies had been left behind to watch for me.

Sure enough, a man in civilian clothes was leaning against my car, smoking a cigarette. Country-and-western music blared from the radio of his pickup truck parked nearby. Sheriff Kutler had either hired an off-duty deputy or one of his red-neck buddies to assist him in this off-the-book caper.

As I contemplated what to do next, the two-way radio in his hand came to life.

"Yo, this is Darrell." He listened. "Shit, Art, don't you think I'da seen him if he come this way? I ain't no dummy." He listened intently, and I wondered if Art Kutler had decided to tell him that very truth. "Well, fuck you and your mother, too! I don't need any of this shit. Not fer what you're payin' me. You watch your own parking lot, you dirty cocksucker!" He threw the radio into the bushes and stomped over to his truck, then fired it up and peeled out of the parking lot and down the road within seconds.

I waited a few minutes, then walked to my car and drove out of there as fast as I could. I hoped Darrell's anger would hold and that he would not have a change of heart and come back looking for me.

He didn't return, and I drove back to Corvallis without seeing anyone.

June 25, 2005

lay in bed for a long time the next morning, trying to figure out where things stood. For the most part, I had more questions than answers. Although I was relieved that Maxine March was still alive, I had no idea where she was. Also, I was nowhere near to clearing my own name and having my arrest expunged from the records.

As he had been since I met him the year before, Duncan Delgado was at the center of everything. I had no idea what his motives were. Fame? Money? Or was he so deranged that he did not care about even these typical motives.

My problem was that no one seemed to know where he was, and no one in authority seemed to be very interested in finding him. And that was my biggest problem. By covering his tracks so well, he had substituted mine. He had set me up perfectly to take the blame that should have been aimed at him. And he did it out of spite. He did not like the relationship that was developing between me and his former wife, my beloved Maxine. Even though he had dumped her, he could not stand for anyone else to get close to her. Or maybe he was messing with me because I was handy as a scapegoat.

My problem was a big one: how to convince the rest of the world that I was innocent and he was guilty. I had burned my bridges with Angela Pride, my former girlfriend and usual compatriot in matters of investigating crimes. I did not regret the fact that I blew up at her. She had thrown me to the wolves without hearing my side, and I could not forgive her for that.

My only real chance to clear my name rested with my friend Paul Bickford, the special ops officer who had saved my life a few weeks ago and had helped me out of more than one tight spot since we met several years ago. He had tipped me off about the sanitarium. I had to find out what he knew about Delgado.

I reached for the phone and dialed a number I was not sure was even current. It rang five times before the voice mail system kicked in.

"Knickerbocker Consultants is not open today. Please leave your name and number, and someone will call you," said the recorded voice of a woman.

Knickerbocker Consultants—his new cover name.

"Is this the party to whom I am speaking," I said, in the nasal-sounding voice of the old Lily Tomlin telephone operator routine. "Professor Martindale would like you to return his call at his residence on a matter of grave importance."

I hung up and got out of bed. After showering and dressing, I made myself some coffee and oatmeal. I read the morning paper as I ate breakfast. The phone rang as I was clearing the table.

"That was fast, Paul. You must be . . ."

"Tom, it's Lorenzo Madrid."

"Sorry, Lorenzo. I thought you were a friend I just tried to reach."

"No problem. First of all, how are you? It must be good to be back among the free."

"You can say that again! I'm feeling a lot better after some sleep and a couple of showers, but it's hard to get rid of that jail stink."

"Yeah, I know what you mean. It's got to be real hard for someone like you to cope with being in jail, even just overnight. Some of my clients are like you—innocent. Others don't bat an eye about being there and just add another tattoo."

"*That* I did not do," I laughed. "I couldn't decide on the design."

"I need to see you as soon as possible," he said. "How about today at 2 P.M. My office."

"I'll be there. Do you have some news for me?"

"I'd rather wait until we can talk face-to-face."

My stomach started churning. "Nothing bad, I hope, like I'm about to be rearrested."

"No, my friend, not that. Just some interesting developments."

After I cleaned up the kitchen, I checked my computer for e-mail messages. I had already dealt with the ones that had accumulated during my time in jail, but saw that thirty more had come in overnight. Where was my spam filter when I needed it?

A new message popped up that I would want to read. It was from Hadley Collins, the vice president for university relations. I had worked with her on a number of special assignments over the years. This was the first message I had gotten from anyone on campus since my release.

> *Tom—I hope this finds you rested and on the mend. I know you have been through a terrible ordeal. I want you to know that there are people on campus who care about you. In fact, I am writing to ask if you could do something for me as soon as possible. Please call at your earliest convenience. Hadley*

I dialed her number from memory.

"Vice President Collins's office, Nancy Plumb speaking."

"This is Public Enemy Number 1. How are you, Nancy?"

"Oh, Tom, I was so worried about you. Are you okay?"

I was touched by the tone of voice of this normally wise-cracking woman whom I have known for years. "Bloodied but unbowed. We need to have coffee, and I will tell you all about it. Thanks for your concern. It means a lot."

"We've got a date. I've never consorted with a felon before. I'll put you through to the vice president."

"Tom, I'm glad you called me so quickly. I was not sure you were even in town," Hadley said, when she got on the line.

"Yeah, I've been sticking around the area. I did go to my place in Newport for a few days. I am in limbo right now. Not sure what to do next. My tenure protects my position, but is it a position worth having? I can imagine what people must think of me. I'm not sure I can stand the whisper campaign that is sure to come." I hoped I wasn't sounding whiny.

"In the first place, you were released without bail. The paper said the person you were accused of killing is not dead?"

"Yeah, it looks that way. But no one knows where she is. The prosecution could not prove that she was dead, so my attorney argued successfully that I could not be held for the murder of someone who was not dead. His argument worked for now, but this isn't over by a long shot. It needs to be cleared up—hopefully before school starts in the fall."

"When that happens, I am sure things will right themselves. We'll have to see that your story is told in the right places. I can help you. I will put the resources of the university's information office at your disposal."

"You would do that?"

"Of course, Tom. You mean a lot to this place. We won't hang you out to dry. I promise you that. I have spoken to President White about you. She remembers you from the committee interviews and the terrible day at the stadium. She's aware of all your hard work for the university over the years."

A few weeks before, two of the candidates for president had been shot by a deranged student during the commencement ceremony in the campus football stadium. Lillian White had not been hit.

I was touched by what Hadley had said. Although I had been on the search committee that recommended White as president, I didn't think she knew anything about me. I figured I was just another face around the conference table. It was gratifying to think that I still might have a career there.

"Hadley, I hardly know what to say. I thought . . . I'd never . . ."

"But that's not why I called." Mercifully, Hadley was changing the subject.

"It's not?"

"No, I need your help on something else. Just a minute while I close the door." I heard her put down the phone and then the door to her office slam shut. "That's better. Nancy will be mad that she can't hear what we're talking about, but I'll fill her in later. This will all sound strange to you, and it is. But here goes. One of my many assignments here on campus is chair of the University Museum Committee. You know the old facility has been closed for a few years while we try to find a new home for it off campus. It's been in the basement of the basketball coliseum, but we need that space now."

"Yeah, I know the museum. I knew one of the last directors and found interns for her to work on PR projects. Do you need that kind of help?"

"No, Tom, nothing like that. We're missing one of the items in the collection."

"Oh, I see." This was beginning to sound strange. "Some of those old Native American baskets? They must be valuable."

"No, a lot larger than those."

"The stagecoach. Now, how did someone steal that?" I knew a bit about that. My boss had helped the museum get the old coach from the family who owned it.

"You promise not to laugh?"

"I promise."

"It's the moose. Some alum shot it on a trip to Alaska in the 1930s, and it has been a popular part of our collection for years. It's been looking a bit tacky lately, but it's our moose and we like it a lot."

"I have always been partial to him—it is a him, I guess."

"Yes. The antlers. Don't forgot the antlers."

"Oh, yes, of course. How could I not remember them."

Hadley was laughing, but I could tell that she was taking this seriously.

"So, the moose is missing. Obviously, some fraternity guy did it. Some kind of prank or an initiation ritual."

"They say no, and I tend to believe them. For one thing, school is out and there are very few students around. We're not sure who took it, only that it is missing. A security guard noticed some straw in front of the door to one of the storage rooms. When he went in, nothing looked out of place at first glance. I mean, we have sixty thousand items, so little stuff could be gone. After he walked through the room, it suddenly dawned on him that the moose was missing. It had been placed in a corner not visible from the doorway, and it was gone."

"Have you brought in the Oregon State Police or the Corvallis police?"

"Not yet. I've been trying to avoid that."

"What is the value of this moose?"

"Like the ad says, priceless."

The whole subject was funny, but no one was laughing.

"It's not the monetary value, Tom. There are other factors to consider here. That's why I've held back on calling the police. In the first place, public knowledge of the theft will make us a laughingstock. I can just see it becoming Jay Leno's punch line or a part of that soft news segment at the end of TV newscasts all over the country. *That* I do not need. My job is to enhance the university's image, not detract from it."

"Yeah, I see your point."

"And there is another element here. The family that donated the moose to us is a prominent Oregon farm family. They've given millions to Oregon University over the years. I would rather they not know about this—at least until Mr. Moose is back in his proper place in the storage room."

"Yeah, I see your point. It would not look good. So, you want me to handle this as a special assignment?" I was being funny, but I could see that Hadley was serious. And I also knew that I would do anything to repay her for supporting me through my current ordeal. "You know I will do whatever you want. I've never been able to turn you down, and I'm not very busy now anyway."

"Good. I figured you would help me. Can you meet me at the museum warehouse in one hour?"

"Okay. Sure. Obviously, there is some urgency here."

"It's summer, Tom. News is slow, so I'm thinking this would get big play if it was discovered. It would attract attention from the Portland station and then be picked up by the networks and CNN. I want you to find him fast."

"Does Mr. Moose have a name?"

She ignored my question. "I'll see you at the warehouse, Tom. It is across the railroad tracks near the printing plant."

* * * * *

Hadley Collins was waiting for me at the door of the warehouse. "No prison pallor?" she said, as she hugged me.

"I am heavily made up," I said, with a deadpan look on my face.

She laughed and led the way to the main door. I followed her into a cavernous space. A tall woman wearing Western garb walked over to meet us. Her grip was stronger than most of the men I've shook hands with.

"Glad to meet you, professor. Glad to meet you." She kept pumping my arm up and down for a full minute.

"Tom, this is Maud Baxter. She's the director of the museum."

"I'm older than most of these exhibits," she said, "but no one else wanted the job, so I'm here until Hadley raises the money for our new home. Then I'll go back to my ranch in eastern Oregon."

"Maud is a descendant of John Horner, the Oregon Agricultural College history professor who started collecting artifacts for the museum in 1923."

"I remember reading about him when I did some background research on the museum about ten years ago."

"Tom enlisted students to work as interns here," said Hadley.

"That's mighty good and mighty nice of you," said Maud.

"Mr. Horner was quite a fellow as I recall," I said.

"He was that. He was one of your original big men on campus. He not only taught all those years, but he set up this place. When he died in 1933, the *Gazette-Times* ran a long story with the headline *END WRITTEN FOR DR. J. B. HORNER.* Coverage was so dramatic in those days. It was said that hundreds of people attended his funeral. William Jasper Kerr himself delivered the eulogy."

Kerr was legendary as the longtime president of the university when it was a college. He later was chancellor of the entire state system of higher education. Students in the years since have studied and checked books out of the main campus library bearing his name.

She handed me a copy of a photo of Horner, dressed in a frock coat and wearing a fedora. He looked like a diplomat at the peace conference which ended World War I at Versailles.

"Mighty important man and I'm mighty proud to have some of his blood in my veins," said Maud. "Mighty proud."

A rather dour-looking woman with frizzy red hair who was standing behind Maud cleared her throat. She had not said a word up to this point.

"Oh, yes. Tom, this is my assistant . . ."

"Excuse me, Miss Baxter, but I am the assistant director, not really your assistant."

"Yes, of course. This is Valerie Pitt, the assistant director of the museum."

The woman nodded, but did not offer me her hand when I stuck out my own.

"Miss Pitt is the academic end of this outfit," continued Maud. "She keeps us honest."

"I make certain that the rules of museum acquisition are followed and that the provenance is accurate," said Pitt.

"I'm sure you do," I said.

"I hold degrees from the University of Akron, and I had a summer internship at the Henry Ford Museum in Michigan," said Pitt, proudly.

Maud appeared to brush the younger woman off and turned to Hadley and me. "I was saying about John Horner . . ."

"A somewhat minor historical figure," said Pitt, haughtily, "and someone we might give too much attention to."

"Dr. Pitt, I think we should air our differences on my ancestor and the way I run this museum in private," continued Maud. "These people are busy."

Hadley was looking a bit impatient. She was always on the way to—or late for—a meeting. "Please show us the room where the moose was kept," said Hadley.

"You bet I will," said Maud, taking off across the large expanse in long strides that were difficult to keep up with. Valerie Pitt disappeared.

Maud led us into an adjacent room with a high ceiling. It was lined with large bins into which had been placed some of the bigger artifacts from the collection: furniture, weaponry, framed paintings, undressed mannequins, and wildlife specimens.

"It would have been more of a scandal if that beaver over there had been filched," she chortled. "That would have narrowed the suspects to some Ducks from down the road."

The mascot of Oregon University was the beaver, and its biggest rival was the University of Oregon, whose mascot is the duck.

We walked around the set for a pioneer cabin, and she stopped at the only empty space on the crowded floor.

"This is where he stood since we brought him over," she said. "Funny not to see him here. I kind of miss him. He was ugly as sin, but he was a part of this place."

Both Maud and Hadley looked at me expectantly, as if they figured I would say something detective-like. I looked around in a vain attempt to find something to react to.

Nothing.

"Maud, can you think of anyone who would have a reason to take the moose? Anyone around here acting suspiciously or eying him?" The question sounded pretty dumb, but by the looks on their faces, both women were taking it seriously.

"Not that I can recall," she said. "I mean, the public hadn't seen him for over a year, since we closed the museum and put everything into storage. Even then, only little kids seemed to notice him—I guess because he was so big and so ugly." Then, Maud Baxter started to cry. This woman had seemed so self-assured and tough up to this point, her tears surprised me.

Hadley Collins moved over and put her arm around Maud's shoulders. "I know it's hard," she said softly. "Tom will find your moose."

Although I had no choice but to help her, I'd planned to spend the next few months on other things—like clearing myself of a murder charge. What did I know about finding a missing moose?

I walked over to the edge of the pioneer room set and did something detective-like: I lifted up the threadbare carpet. Only dust wafted back at me. I entered the room and opened drawers on some of the furniture pieces. All were empty. I was running out of ideas.

"Who has been in here in the past few weeks?"

Maud consulted a logbook she had brought along. "Only our curator staff while they were packing things for the move. We had a guy in to take video footage of the shelves and some of the more valuable items, which I found and arranged for him."

"Who did that work for you?"

Hadley answered my question. "One of your colleagues in journalism, Randy Webb. When I hired him for this job, we talked about you. He said you'd been colleagues for years."

"That we have," I replied. "I trust him completely. Randy's not your guy."

"Then, of course, there's our board of directors," added Maud Baxter. "They were here just last week to look things over. We are relying on them for some of the fundraising."

"Do you have a list of their names?"

"I figured you want to see it," said Maud, as she pulled it out from under some other papers on her clipboard. "Here you are."

Along with the names of off-campus people who I assumed had money, the name of the vice-chair leapt out at me: *Duncan Delgado.*

elgado!" I exclaimed. Although I could not think of any earthly reason for Duncan Delgado to steal a moth-eaten moose, I knew he had done it the minute I saw his name on the list. Why? I could not guess. Now Hadley's request that I find the taxidermied treasure did not seem farfetched at all. It was one piece of a puzzle I was determined to solve.

"Tom, are you with us?" Hadley was speaking, but I had not heard what she said.

"Sorry, Hadley. I was just thinking . . ."

"Do you know Delgado?"

"Er . . . a . . . I've met him. We were almost on jury duty together last year."

"Wasn't your friend, Ms. March, married to him?"

"Yes, she was."

"I thought I remembered that."

I turned to Maud Baxter, who was straightening the doilies in the pioneer room display. "Miss Baxter . . ."

"Call me Maud. My friends all do!"

"Maud, tell me exactly how Dr. Delgado happened to be here and what he did."

"Sure, Tom, I'm glad to do that. Well, the board members were all here for the quarterly luncheon we host to bring them up to date on fund raising and any stuff we need to have them vote on. I was surprised to see Dr. Delgado here. He had only attended one other meeting in the year he had been on the board. I suppose he got placed on the committee by his department chair and was not all that interested in what we do."

"That happens a lot," said Hadley. "We tolerate it because we need senior people to serve on committees, not just faculty members who are on the way up and need it for their resumes."

"Yeah, I've been guilty of that myself," I confessed.

Maud was now getting impatient with the two of us and cleared her throat to get our attention. "To continue my story. Well sir, so Dr. Delgado shows up and takes a real interest in things and asks a lot of questions about the scientific exhibits we have here. Seemed even to want to help get some grant money to improve them." She looked around conspiratorially and lowered her voice. "They aren't very good. So, my old ears perked up, and I listened to him real good."

"Did he offer to write a grant request?"

"He offered, and I got him the information he asked for on the contents of the exhibits and the provenance of the items." As an aside, she confided, "That's the information on who gives us what and why and how old it is."

Both Hadley and I nodded.

"But I never saw anything he did, and he would never give me a straight answer as to whether he did send anything in."

"Did the moose play a role in anything he proposed?"

"Now that you mention it, he worked the discussion around to our collection of specimens. He did this early on and asked to see them. So I gathered them together in one spot so he could look at them. He paid no attention to the birds and smaller critters, like the squirrels and moles. Even the beaver did not catch his eye."

"He was interested in bigger mammals?" I suggested, knowing the answer to my question already.

"You bet he was!" she said. "He liked the wolf and the coyote and the black bear."

"And the moose, of course," said Hadley, picking up the drift of the conversation.

"Oh, yes. Now that you mention it, Dr. Delgado seemed really fond of that moose," Maud said. "He looked him over pretty good and even got up on a ladder to examine his antlers. He mentioned that he might see if we could get him reconditioned."

"You mean, restuffed?" I asked.

"Yes, sir, he was looking pretty tacky. The straw was coming out here and there. They use more modern kinds of stuffing now, I believe. Dr. Delgado mentioned that it would be easy to get funds to redo all the big animal specimens. And I was all ears. No one had ever said a word about doing anything like that before."

"Did he say anything about removing the animals to do this?"

"He did not get specific, but he asked how he could gain access to this area, in case he got the money to pay for the work."

"So you gave him a key?"

"No, we have a code setup on the doors. I gave him the code."

Hadley and I looked at one another, and Maud Baxter's face turned red.

"So I guess I handed him our moose on a silver platter, so to speak." She shook her head. "How could I have been so dumb?"

Hadley moved to comfort her again. "It's not your fault, Maud," she said. "How could you know that a board member was planning to steal your prized possession."

"This guy is good, believe me," I added. "He's turned my life upside down without much trouble. The problem is proving it."

"And why would he want a moth-eaten old moose?" said Hadley, glancing at Maud Baxter for fear she had hurt her feelings.

"I don't have a clue," I said, "but I intend to find out." I turned to Maud. "How long after you gave him the combination code to the door did the moose disappear?"

"About a week, I think."

"So he had plenty of time to plan how to get the moose out and find a place to stash him." I thought for a moment. "I think I know just where that might be."

Hadley and Maud looked at me questioningly.

"Better if you not know. I will be in touch." I walked out the door and was in my car in seconds.

Although my first instinct was to drive out to the Animal Isolation Lab on the edge of campus, I decided that I would have to put that off until dark. I wouldn't gain a thing by going there now, only a secretary telling me that Delgado was out of town. If he was still in town, me showing up there would tip him off that I was digging into his affairs once again. I was hoping to keep him from hearing that I was out of jail, at least for a few more days. Besides, I had an appointment in Salem with my attorney, Lorenzo Madrid.

*   *   *   *   *

Unlike my first visit to Madrid's office over a year ago, the waiting room was empty. The other time it had been filled with the men, women, and children he was helping with their immigration problems. I walked in the door, but found no one on duty at the reception desk. I pushed down on the bell—like one of those at the front desk of hotels—once.

Within seconds, Madrid stuck his head out of the door to the rear and walked out to greet me.

"*Mi amigo,*" he said, embracing me. I returned the hug. "Come on back," he said. "I want you to meet someone."

I followed him down a hall to his small office at the rear of the building. He motioned me through the door.

"Tom Martindale, I'd like you to meet Raymond Pearl."

An older man got up and held out his hand, which I shook. He looked like a broken-down prizefighter, with a nose that was slightly off-center and a red face that was deeply lined. He wore his thinning hair in a massive comb-over that was plastered down with so much hairspray that it would not have moved even in hurricane-force winds.

"Glad to meet ya, fella," he said in a heavy Brooklyn accent.

"Sit down, Tom," said Madrid.

"I'm anxious to hear what you've found out," I said. "Did you come up with something to clear me?"

"Nothing conclusive yet, but I'm confident we'll wrap this up soon. First, let me say again, there is no doubt in my mind that you got railroaded. No doubt. Not sure who was behind it, though. I think people just jumped to some very bad conclusions. You got caught in the system. Most of the time when that happens, people get swallowed up and that's that. Fortunately, we got lucky."

"Boy, luck or your skill or whatever it was, I am grateful."

"Now we've got to get this taken care of permanently, so you won't be looking over your shoulder for the rest of your life. I asked you to come over to meet Ray. I mentioned before that he's been my investigator for a few years, and he is the best."

Pearl smiled and nodded as only a New Yorker would. No false modesty here. He truly believed that he was the best—and I hoped so, too.

"Ray, tell Tom what you found out."

Pearl cleared his throat, put on his glasses, and opened a small notebook. With the glasses perched on the end of his nose, he looked slightly professorial. "Professor, Lorenzo hired me to look into your case, and here's what I've found so far." He cleared his throat again. "First of all, your relationship with this gal . . ."

"Maxine March," I interjected. "Her name was Maxine March."

"Yeah, yeah. Whatever. Anyways, it was pretty innocent. You didn't even date all that much. You may have lusted after her in your heart, but you never lusted after her in her bedroom."

I didn't react to his bluntness but merely nodded, deciding not to state the obvious. I had not lied to Madrid or anyone else.

"Second of all, you was right in your feelin' that this Delgado guy is bad news. He stinks to high heaven in lots of what he has done in his life. He screwed a lot of people—both literally and figuratively—on his way up the ladder of life. Lots of times he gained by making someone else lose—big time! It's all here in my report, so I won't bore you with it now. Just know that it is all there. In short, he wants what he wants, and he'll do anything to get it! He took your friend Maxine on a wild ride. Married her and then dumped her and then fought her all the way about alimony and stuff like that. He seems to have stepped in from time to time to get her fired from jobs and even to interfere with her boyfriends.

"He is a real piece of work. I mean to say, he is a real piece of shit when it comes to how he treated her and all the women who have been in his life. And he's had his share. He's a real lover boy, but his pattern is a few nights in the sack and then he dumps 'em. And he don't stick to one social class. I mean, there's been secretaries and grad students and a dean's wife or two or three." Pearl looked me in the eye, and Madrid nodded for him to continue. "I did some digging around the medical examiner's office and got ahold of the DNA results of the body everyone said was your friend."

Based on the report that she might have been at the sanitarium, I knew he was going to say that it wasn't Maxine, but I kept that to myself until he was finished.

"It ain't her. It's some Mexican gal . . . ," he glanced at another piece of paper, "Margarita Santoro." He looked at me. "You ever heard that name before?"

I shook my head. "No, never."

"We got only a name and an ID from her Mexican driver's license. We traced her through dental records. I called in a favor from some friends in the local police down there. She's from Oaxaca in southern Mexico. Probably illegal."

"Probably one of the people he brought up as research subjects," I said. I turned to Madrid. "The people I saw that night in the lab. I met another one just yesterday, a young Mexican woman and her son. Delgado has them staying at an abandoned sanitarium in the Coast Range. She told me she saw him escort a woman out of the building and drive away with her. It has to have been Maxine, although we can't know for certain."

"Why didn't you tell us?" Pearl asked me. Then turning to Madrid, "He's got to level with us if this is going to work."

"I was getting to that, but I wanted to hear your report." I said.

"Jesus!" said Pearl, shaking his head.

"That is good news, Tom," said Madrid, ignoring his investigator. "Now we've just got to find her. Have you got anything else, Ray?"

"Yeah, a little bit more that's pretty int-restin'," said Pearl, again consulting his notebook. "Back to Delgado and the gal who everyone thought was your friend. So he kills her and batters her head in so she is unrecognizable and then plants your faculty ID card on the body, figuring that everyone would leap to the conclusion that you did it before checking. And, you know what? It worked. Justice can be swift, especially if it's in the hands of zealots."

"Amen to that," I muttered.

"But, since then, Delgado has done a pretty good job of hiding your friend. We ain't found no trace of her," said Pearl. "She just plain vanished. The poor kid's probably scared shitless all the time. I mean, she knows this guy and what he is capable of doin'. He is one bad guy."

"We need to find her and bring her into court to prove your innocence," said Madrid. "That will put the facts behind the picture I conjured up out of thin air—I mean, that there was no proof that Maxine March was dead. The judge bought it, but I certainly wasn't sure it was right. I am as relieved as you are that she is alive, but for different reasons."

He turned to Pearl. "Is that it, Ray? Do you have anything more?"

The investigator shook his head. "Naw. That's it."

"You did a great job," I said. "Thanks a lot."

"That's what Lorenzo pays me the big bucks to do," he laughed.

"You were going to tell us about this abandoned sanitarium, Tom?" said Madrid.

"It's pretty bizarre, but it's all true," I said. And then I told them about Ocean Springs Sanitarium and my time there, about Maria and Ronaldito, and the whole spooky place. "It got dark and three or four guys—sheriff's deputies—with dogs arrived, so I got out of there."

"You left the woman and the boy there?" said Madrid.

"I had nowhere to take them and, if it was the sheriff, my presence would only make it worse. He'd try to blame me for taking them into the country or some other crime he would dream up."

"Your old nemesis from the jail, the sheriff from the coast?" asked Madrid.

"Yeah, Art Kutler. You met him. He's a real jerk."

"But why was he lookin' for you?" asked Pearl.

"I doubt that he was—maybe he just had the place staked out for some other reason. I know him, though. Finding me there would be all he'd need to pin all the unsolved crimes in the county on me."

"He really hates you that much?" asked Pearl.

"He really hates me that much," I nodded, ruefully. "I figured Maria and her son were doing okay on their own. I think they are expert at hiding out from whoever shows up. But I know they are illegal, and they can't stay there indefinitely."

"You're right, Tom," said Madrid. "We've got to get them out of there to someplace safe. I think you need to take us out to that sanitarium."

"You might have missed some clues," said Pearl. "I mean, with all due respect to your intelligence, you are an amateur. No offense." He held out his hands palms up, in a defensive stance.

"None taken," I said. "It will be nice to have some reinforcements when I go out there. I am sick of doing this kind of stuff alone. I need you guys."

"Agreed," said Madrid. "We'll go tomorrow. I'll take a social worker with us to help with Maria and her son. You'll like her. Her name is Treena Martin. She's Anglo, but very skilled in these kinds of situations. And she speaks Spanish like a native. I'll give her a call."

"I'll try to find out some more about our friend Delgado," said Pearl. "He's probably gone into hiding. Looks like he's not in

Europe like his office girl said, so he's got to be around here, hiding in plain sight."

"Legally, he's got nothing to worry about," said Madrid. "I mean, the police are not looking for him. It's summer, so he can be away from campus without arousing any suspicion. Best we not tip him off that we are nosing into his activities."

Madrid turned to me. "By the way, Tom, I forgot to ask how you found out about the sanitarium in the first place. Why'd you go there?"

"My friend Paul Bickford put me on to it. He suggested I check it out, but didn't tell me why."

"Do you think he'd be able to find out more about Delgado than we've been able to do?"

"Probably," I said. "He's got the resources of the whole federal government, if he chooses to use them."

"Is he some kind of secret agent?" asked Pearl. "So he just drops that little fact on you about this nut house and then takes a powder?"

"That's his pattern," I said, shaking my head, explaining his job in Army Special Ops. "I've known him for several years—he's like some kind of cunning animal. One minute he's there, the next he's gone."

"Well, keep trying to get in touch with him," said Madrid. "We need to know if he knows where Maxine is and, if so, get his help to bring her to Oregon and testify that she's alive."

"I'll call when I get home and keep calling. He almost always helps me, but he often uses national security as the excuse when he can't."

"I don't see that this has any connection with national security," said Madrid. "It's a homicide investigation."

"Unless you count Delgado's research on Ebola and his plan to use human subjects like Maria to do it," I said. "If he's using a live virus and it gets into the wrong hands, a lot of people will get infected and die."

"But I thought he was trying to advance his career by finding a cure for that virus," said Madrid.

"He is, but he's nutty enough to turn that around and sell the cure and any toxins he has to the highest bidder," I said.

Madrid stood up. "I've got some clients in the waiting room. Let's meet in the parking lot of the Burgerville Restaurant in Monmouth at 9 A.M. tomorrow. We can all go in my Jeep to this sanitarium of yours, Tom. I'll try to find us a quicker way in. I know a guy who hunts up in the Coast Range all the time. He'll know about this place, I am sure, and can give me a good route."

Pearl and I stood up, and we all shook hands.

"I feel better with you two helping me."

"Wait'll ya get my bill," laughed Pearl. "Just kiddin'."

"One thing, though," said Madrid, catching me by the arm as I walked out of his office. "Just go home and rest. Don't go off on your own. Wait until we all go up to the sanitarium tomorrow. Promise me?"

"Lorenzo, I have no intention of going up to that place alone again." But I didn't promise to stay home and rest.

We all parted in his waiting area, which by now was full of his clients. I waved to Pearl as I drove away. I figured I would wait until after dark to return to the Animal Isolation Lab. Although I had no proof, I felt it held answers to my questions about Maxine and even the missing moose.

s I had done a few weeks before, I decided to wait until dark to go to the Animal Isolation Lab at the edge of campus. While I was waiting to drive out there, I looked up basic information on the university Web site to see if anything had changed.

Much to my surprise, I discovered that Duncan Delgado was now its director. The last time I was there, another man was in charge. But he had a badly broken leg, so maybe he had to give up his post. As second in command, Delgado was the logical person to take over. I shook my head. The man led a charmed life. Nothing bad ever stuck to him.

Once again I parked my car on the main campus near the University Theatre and walked along a path by the cow and sheep barns and over the covered bridge. It was a warm night and I enjoyed my journey, despite what I was on my way to do: break into a restricted university lab.

I arrived at the line of trees on the hill above the lab at about 9 P.M. The floodlights illuminated the building below, and I intended to watch for a long time before making my move.

From my vantage point, I could see a single security guard sitting at a desk in the small office at the front of the building. From before, I remembered that was the only entrance. In the daytime, a receptionist sits where the guard was sitting, and the offices for secretaries, the director, and other staff members were in the back. There were a few lab rooms on the main floor, but the area I was heading for was in the basement, reached only via a steep wooden ladder. That was where I had found the migrants before; that was where I was compelled to go now.

At 9:30 P.M., I walked down the hill to the fence and turned left. I was hoping to find an opening somewhere along its perimeter, since I knew from my visit here before that it was not electrified.

I rounded the corner and walked along the long expanse behind the building. No opening of any kind. I came around the other side and spied what I had been looking for. A natural creek bed ran under the fence. At this time of year, with no water flowing in it, the space between the straight line of the fence and the bottom of the creek made an opening that a person might crawl through. At least, that is what I hoped.

I sprawled out on the ground and wiggled under the fence. Things went fine until my pants snagged on one of the loops of the chain link. I moved back and forth for a time, but the effort only seemed to ensnare me more.

I reached around and found the culprit: a belt loop on my jeans. As I tried to unhook my jeans, I heard the door of the office open. Then I heard the gravel crunching under the guard's boots.

My heart raced as I willed myself into invisibility. I hoped the indentation of the creek bed would shield me, at least partially. He kept coming toward me, so I just kept my head down and remained quiet. The crunching continued.

"What the hell?" he muttered, at a point only a few hundred yards away from where I was. He had seen me for sure!

"God damn glasses," he said.

I ventured a peek just in time to see him bend down and pick up his eyeglasses, which must have fallen onto the ground. Apparently, he had then stepped on them and broken at least one lens. I relaxed as he went back in the other direction, still muttering.

With the guard back at his post inside, I reached into my pocket for the small knife I usually carry. I seldom use it, but carry it as a good luck charm. It had belonged to my grandfather. I opened it and carefully used the blade to start sawing away at the belt loop. After what seemed like a long time, I managed to cut the threads on the loop, and it pulled away from the waistband of the jeans. With this obstruction removed, I easily slid under the fence, then I got to my feet and ran toward the edge of the building, out of the floodlights.

I crept back toward the windows of the office and glanced in to see the guard, now without his glasses, munching on an apple and squinting at a copy of The National Enquirer. As he contemplated the next scandal involving the Clintons or Britney Spears, accompanied by brutally frank photos of Oprah between diets and without makeup, I ran over to the gate and rattled it as hard as I could. The noise reverberated along the fence line. Then I ran back into the shadow of the building.

The guard looked up from his magazine and came to the doorway. Without his glasses, he was quite nearsighted. He squinted toward the noise and walked in the direction of the gate. With this back turned, I slipped in through the open door and through the waiting area to the hallway behind. I closed that door and quickly ran to the office that had been Delgado's before. The sign on the door now said Conference Room. I stepped inside without turning on the lights.

Aided by the floodlights shining through the windows, I could see the familiar bookshelves and a large table surrounded by chairs. Even though Delgado had moved into the director's office down the hall, he still kept a computer and printer in this room. As I had before, I found a key taped to the back of the printer. I pulled on the bookshelves, and they opened like the double doors of a closet. Behind the shelves was a narrow door held in place by a large padlock. I used the key to open it and then stepped into a small room lined with filing cabinets. At the far end of this room, I again found the trapdoor at the top of the ladder leading to the floor below.

I shined my small penlight onto the ladder and began my descent. As I reached the dirt floor below, I smelled the mixture of human sweat and animal waste that I remembered from my last time here. As I expected, the small, gruesome rooms where the monkeys had been kept were empty.

Thank God for small favors. I had heard that some animals had been destroyed and others were being kept in isolation until their health status was determined.

How had Delgado kept his job and even been promoted after that scandal had been revealed? I hoped that an investigation was planned, although I had not heard of one. Delgado's record of bringing in large grants must be protecting him for now. How would a murder charge or two affect his career? He would not be able to squirm out of that!

I walked to the end of the passageway to the room where people had been housed. The smell was not as bad in here, although I had the urge to flee as soon as I entered. I turned on the single light, a bare bulb hanging from the ceiling in the middle of the room.

Bunks lined the walls and a wooden table and some benches stood in the center of the room. A small wood-burning stove sat on a platform of bricks at the far end. I peeked into a tiny room near the stove and found a chemical toilet and single water tap. Delgado had not exactly renovated this space to make his guests comfortable!

Someone had made an attempt to sweep the floor and then dumped everything into a large trash can. The dustpan and broom were leaning up against it. Fearing something truly distasteful, I peered into the can hesitantly and saw what looked like dirt and papers in the bottom. Because the can was too heavy to lift, I pulled it onto its side and pulled the contents out onto the floor. I used the broom as a prod to move the contents around.

Wrappers from fast food and empty cups dominated the assemblage of debris. Torn pages from a children's book, in Spanish, were also there, plus a map of the California/Mexico border. A yellow marker had been used to trace a route through the desert east of San Diego. I wiped it off and put it in my pocket.

In all the other depressing remnants of the time the small band of migrants had rested here, I almost missed a crumpled up paper. I put it on the table and smoothed it out.

It was a photo of the beach below my house in Newport with the Yaquina Head Lighthouse in the background. Maxine March had taken it a year ago, soon after I first met her; I suppose she could have taken the shot before we met that day. She had followed me there and been quite forward in telling me she wanted to get to know me better. I had resisted her advances and sent her on her way. I turned the photo over. *Tom's house in Newport* was written on the back in her neat handwriting.

I was happy to find more evidence that Maxine was alive. I put the photo in my pocket and used the broom to shove the debris back into the can, lifting it upright again. I turned out the light and walked back into the passageway.

There was one last room to check—one I had not looked into on my first visit here. It was to the right of the room where the people had been housed. I opened the door and stepped in. It had a cement floor and was in a bit better shape than the rest of the basement. It was also a lot bigger than the others down here, with a high ceiling and a garage-type door to the outside.

The room contained both bookshelves and filing cabinets. It was probably an area where Delgado could work near his research subjects—both human and simian. Everything had been cleared away now. The shelves were empty. I pulled out the drawers and they were equally barren. They rattled loudly as I opened and closed them.

As I started to leave, I noticed a substance on the floor that was barely visible from under the overhang on one of the bookshelves. I bent down to examine it more closely.

It appeared to be cleanser, but why would it be here? There was no sink to clean on this entire level. I turned away to leave, then stopped. I knelt down and wetted the end of one finger, then I dabbed it in the substance and smelled the glob I retrieved.

What greeted my nostrils was not the odor of disinfectant I had expected but a substance with a strong chemical smell. While I was no expert, it was fairly clear what this stuff was: cocaine.

I bent down more closely and saw that small piles of it were lying all along this side of the baseboard. At the corner, I noticed something of a yellowish brown color. I picked it up and dropped it in my hand. The straw was so old that it disintegrated in my hand as soon as I touched it.

At that point I knew why Delgado had taken the moose and how he had financed his elaborate research scheme.

June 26, 2005

As I drove up Highway 99W toward Monmouth the next morning, I thought about my discovery the night before. Delgado must be using the moose as a way to transport the cocaine he needed to finance his research into the Ebola virus. Wild as it sounded, he had stolen the old stuffed moose from the museum, removed the straw filling, and filled it with cocaine he had obtained from connections he had in Mexico—maybe the same people who helped him bring in the migrants. Then, he had brought the moose into Oregon and sold the cocaine. The details were confusing, but I knew he had done it. The difficulty would be in proving it.

I was not clear about Maxine's involvement. She probably had no connection to any of it, but might know enough that he needed to keep her quiet. The basement of the lab and the sanitarium were good temporary locations, but where was she now?

Madrid, Pearl, and an attractive woman in her thirties stood beside a Jeep in the parking lot of the Burgerville as I drove in.

"You may want to park on the street," said Madrid, "since you're leaving your car for a while." He gestured toward the adjacent street. I followed his advice and parked under a tree before joining them next to Madrid's car.

"Tom, this is Treena Martin. Treena, Tom."

"Hi," she smiled. "Lorenzo has told me all about you."

We shook hands.

"Morning, Ray," I said to Pearl, shaking his hand, too.

"Let's get going," said Madrid. "We've got a lot to do today."

We all got into the Jeep and Lorenzo drove out of the parking lot. He headed due west past the campus of Western Oregon University and out into the country.

"We'll go through Falls City, then loop around on some logging roads a friend told me about," he said, as he handed me a forest service map that contained detailed topography of the area.

Although I was eager to tell Madrid about what I had discovered at the lab, I decided to wait until I could get him alone. I did not know Ray or Treena well enough to trust them.

"I had no luck getting ahold of your pal Paul Bickford," said Pearl from the back seat.

I didn't want to admit that I hadn't tried, preoccupied as I was in breaking into the lab. "Me neither," I said. "I'll try again later today."

"Treena here is very good at dealing with people who are scared and frightened," said Madrid, as he half turned in his seat to look at her.

"I've helped Lorenzo with a lot of his clients, especially the illegal ones," she said.

"I don't like to think of them as 'illegals'," he smiled. "Maybe people whose citizenship has just not come through yet."

"That's about as much legal hairsplitting and bullshit as I ever heard," muttered Pearl from behind us.

Madrid smiled. "It's a glass half full/half empty kind of thing," he said.

We drove in silence for a long time and enjoyed the beautiful scenery of the Coast Range in summer. As we left the town and small farms, the road gradually narrowed so that it was lined by tall trees. Here and there, clear-cut areas scarred the landscape. As we drove higher and higher, ridge after ridge appeared ahead of us, most covered in thick forests.

"Really pretty," said Martin. "I miss the outdoors so much."

"You need to get out of Portland more than you do," said Madrid, as he turned again to smile at her. I wasn't sure if their relationship extended to their personal lives, but it was none of my business.

We drove another fifteen minutes in silence before reaching the remains of Valsetz, the abandoned timber town that had all but vanished. He drove ahead to the barricade where I had left my car.

"This is where you headed out, I believe," said Madrid. "Right, Tom?"

"Yes, I went down that path and walked for a mile or so before I reached a ridge. I could see the hospital from there across a small valley."

Madrid opened the map and pointed at one of the narrow lines on it. "I think if we take this old logging road, it will get us across that valley a lot faster than you made it walking, and then we can drive right up to the place from this side," he said, punctuating his words by tapping the map with his finger. "What do you think, Ray?"

"Too much God damn green for me," he muttered. "You get me there, and I'll do my detectin'. Just don't expect me to know the way!"

The three of us smiled, although the grizzled investigator was quite serious.

"Ray is a city guy at heart," laughed Madrid, as he turned left and drove into a thick forest where the road had barely been carved out.

"You got *that* right," came another mutter from the back seat.

As Madrid had predicted, we soon started going downhill into the small valley I had had such trouble getting across before. The Jeep easily forded the streams, and we were soon ascending the other side. Madrid kept looking at the map and soon had us moving north along a road that was easier to navigate because the trees had been cut down.

"I hate clear-cuts," I said. "It ruins everything. Looks like an atom bomb went off."

"Yeah, I agree," said Madrid, "but with the price of timber so high right now, the owners of this land have been cutting like crazy."

Before long, I could see the ruined sanitarium ahead of us. As we drove through the gate, however, I was startled to see two sheriff's cars sitting near the building. I groaned as a familiar figure waddled into view. He put up his hand and Madrid stopped the car.

"You are interfering with sheriff's department business," said the head man himself, Art Kutler. He leaned down and recognized me.

"Well, well, well," he smiled. "My day just got real int-restin'. I want all of you to step out of the car very carefully and keep your hands where I can see them."

"That seems a bit extreme," said Madrid. "We are not violating any laws that I can see. I am an attorney at law and this is my client. Those are my associates." He gestured toward Pearl and Martin in the back seat.

Kutler turned around and signaled for reinforcements. Two deputies walked toward us, their hands on their guns.

"The sheriff and I have a history, as I've told you," I said to Madrid softly. "He hates my guts."

"What you'd say?" said Kutler. "How old and dear friends we were? I'm waitin' for you to obey my lawful order."

Madrid sat for a moment, considering our options.

"I'd do what he says, Lorenzo," I said. "He's unpredictable."

Madrid opened the door and stepped out. I did the same on my side, and then we both lifted the seats to let Pearl and Martin out of the back. We were soon standing in a line facing the three lawmen.

"I know you," Kutler said to Madrid. "I seen you at the jail when you were visitin' my old friend the professor."

"Yes, I remember you very well," said Madrid.

The youngest-looking deputy stepped behind us and began to frisk Pearl. He told Treena Martin to step to the side, away from us.

"I'd advise you to order your man to cease that action," said Madrid. "You do not have probable cause to . . ."

"This ones packin' a gun," said the deputy, as he pulled a small revolver from a holster on Ray Pearl's leg. He handed it to Kutler.

"You got a concealed weapons permit for this?" asked the sheriff.

"In my office safe in Portland," said Pearl.

"Well, that doesn't do us much good today, now does it?" smirked Kutler.

The deputy moved behind me and frisked me as well.

"This one's not packin'," he said to the sheriff.

"Why doesn't that surprise me," said Kutler. "The professor here is more cerebral. He doesn't need a gun to commit crimes."

The deputy moved behind Madrid, who held up both hands. "Sheriff, I am an officer of the court, and I advise you to call your man off. You have no cause to suspect any of us of anything, and if you carry out an unlawful search of my person, I will bring you up on charges. You can bet on that. I know the law, and you know I know the law."

Kutler paused for a moment and seemed in as deep a thought as he was capable of. He even stroked his chin in a contemplative gesture that was laughable. "Okay, counselor, I take your point. Back off, Dale."

The deputy stepped away from the four of us.

"Now, what are you doing here?" the sheriff said to me.

"We are taking a day off and enjoying the great outdoors," Madrid answered for me. "Mr. Pearl and Miss Martin are from Portland, and I am from Salem. Mr. Martindale told me about this interesting old hospital, and we wanted to see it. Pure curiosity brought us here, sheriff."

Kutler smiled again and turned toward the end of the building. "Are you sure it wasn't them?" he said, pointing in that direction.

Another deputy pulled Maria and Ronaldito into view.

"*Ayudanos, señor, por favor,*" shouted Maria.

"By what authority are you arresting these people?" shouted Madrid.

Kutler smiled. "Counselor, my authority comes from this badge." He pointed to the tin star on his shirt. "I don't need nothin' else."

"You need probable cause to detain them in this way. Have they committed a crime?"

"They're as illegal as hell," Kutler laughed. "I don't need nothin' else. You know and I know they are wetbacks."

Madrid got red in the face, but he kept his composure. "I am Hispanic, sheriff. Does that make me, in your outdated terminology, a 'wetback'?"

"Your folks mebbe were," said Kutler, "but you cleaned up a bit and got a few college degrees and here you are, representing your people. I think that's great. But you'll have to wait to help these folks until they get taken to Salem and I turn them over to the Feds, and then they'll take them to God knows where. You know what, counselor? You may never catch up to them."

"So, you are acting as an agent of the Immigration and Naturalization Service, sheriff?" continued Madrid. "Are their names on a watch list? Are they wanted for committing crimes? How do you know they are not legal residents of Oregon?"

Madrid kept his voice steady, but I could tell that he was outraged at Kutler. I had felt that way many times while dealing with him over the years. More than once in the time I had known the sheriff, only his badge had kept me from taking a swing at him. I had usually been able to win my arguments with him easily, however, because of his lack of brain power.

"They had no IDs, and they couldn't speak English. I always say that if these people come here, they should speak English. How do they expect to get along?"

"Do you ever go to Mexico, sheriff?"

"Yeah, me and some buddies go every year to fish in Baja. We have us a great old time." Kutler smiled at the memory.

"I'll bet you do, and I'll bet you are treated well," said Madrid.

"Yes, sir, we are treated good."

"Do you speak Spanish, sheriff?"

"Well, hell no, why should I do that? If those people down there want my bid-ness, they'd sure as hell better be able to understand what I'm sayin'." As he spoke, the two deputies with him nodded their heads in agreement.

"I see your point, sheriff," said Madrid. "But my point is why should these two people be expected to speak English in this country if you don't have the courtesy to speak Spanish when you go to their country?"

"Well . . . er . . . a . . . because we're Amurika, the greatest country on earth, and people from these other pissant places had damn well better know how to talk to us when they come sneakin' in here!"

"Damn right!" said one of his deputies.

"Damn right!" the other one chimed in.

Madrid continued to remain calm and did not react to Kutler's jingoistic outburst. He pulled out his wallet and opened it, before he handed it to the sheriff.

"These credentials prove that I am an officer of the court," he said. "Based on that standing, I am taking custody of these two people. At a time in the immediate future, I will present them before the properly convened authority to determine their immigration status."

"Not in your wildest dreams, counselor," said Kutler. "They ain't leavin' here with anyone but me."

The deputies pulled Maria and Ronaldito closer to the police car.

"Is this an election year, sheriff?"

"What's that got to do with anything?" asked Kutler in a mocking tone. "You gonna be my campaign manager?"

"I'm afraid I'm far too busy for that kind of time commitment, but thanks for asking," answered Madrid. "What I was thinking of was how it would look when it comes out that you spend your time tracking down a poor woman and her cute little son in a remote area and then treating them roughly for no apparent reason. For starters, you have no proof that they have committed a crime. And why are you way out here, when all kinds of bad things might be happening elsewhere in your jurisdiction? People are speeding along the highways. Other people might be robbing houses to pay for their meth habit. Marijuana is being cultivated on acre after acre of land very close to where we are standing now. But here you are, rousting this poor woman and her little boy. The media would love it."

Kutler frowned, no doubt remembering the toll a similar incident took on his career a number of years ago, when his part in blowing up a whale carcass on the beach in Newport became big news.

"What'll you do with 'em?"

"I'll take them to Salem or Portland where they can stay with people who will take care of them until I can determine their status," said Madrid. "They are not criminals, sheriff. They are law-abiding people."

"Cut 'em loose," growled Kutler to his deputies.

The one named Dale looked confused, but eventually cut the plastic ties that were restraining the arms of Maria and Ronaldito. The two rubbed their wrists and walked over toward Madrid.

"*Gracias, señor,*" said Maria, who seemed on the verge of tears. She almost kneeled in front of Madrid, but he prevented her from doing that.

"*Por nada,*" said Madrid. He motioned for them to walk back to Treena Martin, who hugged both Maria and her son and led them to the car.

"You won this round, counselor," said Kutler, grimly. "But I'm gonna be watchin' you to see if you do what you say you'll do with these people. I can go to the media too, ya know."

"Indeed you can, Sheriff Kutler. I welcome your scrutiny. I would want you to go to the media if I screwed up this case. Contrary to what you might think, we attorneys are not infallible. We do make mistakes and need to be called down when we do." Madrid stepped forward and held out his hand. "Can we shake on it, sheriff?"

Kutler contemplated the gesture for a few seconds, then turned around and walked toward his men. "Let's get the hell out of here," he said. "I'm not likin' the smell so much."

Kutler was repeating a pattern I had seen before. When challenged by someone in higher authority or of a higher intelligence level, he usually backed down. As with most small-minded people like him, he didn't know his own limitations. And they were so great!

I had resisted the urge to say anything at all during the exchange between Kutler and Madrid. I was glad that Lorenzo had won so easily. I was also glad that Maria and Ronaldito would not have to spend time in jail, that we could rescue them from Delgado's clutches.

We watched the sheriff and his men move to their cars. When they drove away, Treena Martin led the boy and his mother to the Jeep and gave each a bottle of water.

"Tom, let's you and me and Ray take a quick look around this place," said Madrid.

I led them around the back and in through the kitchen door.

"Jesus!" muttered Pearl. "What a horror show!"

We picked our way through the dark rooms and into the lobby, which was much brighter because of the tall windows. I filled them in on what I knew of the sanitarium and the kinds of diseases that were treated here.

"That was really barbaric to put syphilis sufferers in scalding water until they went into convulsions," said Madrid.

"Show us that tub room," said Pearl. "That, I gotta see."

"Right through here," I said, leading them to that part of the building.

Even in summer, the place felt damp and clammy. The unused slings hung over some of the tubs and swayed gently. The tubs were filthy with the grime of the ages built up on their insides. The odor from a combination of human sweat, urine, and feces mixed with sulfa from the springs was overpowering. We all put our hands over our noses and mouths.

"Jesus!" said Pearl. "How could anyone in his right mind agree to this kind of treatment?"

"I guess desperate people will do anything to get cured of something as bad as syphilis," said Madrid.

"Let's get the hell out of here," said Pearl. "I'm gettin' sick."

We moved quickly back out into the lobby, which had a source of fresh air because of all the broken windows.

"Where's the loony bin?" asked Pearl, when he had recovered. "Where'd they keep the crazies?"

As I had done a few days before, I walked up to the second floor and to the entrance of the psychiatric unit. "I got this far, but as you can see, this section is . . ."

The heavy steel door that had stopped me before was wide open.

The three of us walked slowly though the doorway. Given what we had seen already, this section of the sanitarium was probably worse. The long hall was identical to those on the other floors; the difference was that the doors to these rooms were not open to let any light in.

The doors on each room were made of steel and the small windows in each had no glass in them. Instead, they were covered with thick bars. We fanned out along the hall, and each looked into a different room.

The door to the one I picked was locked. Through the small window, I could see another window in the outer wall, which was also covered with bars and frosted glass with wire mesh imbedded in it.

"Jesus, Mary, and Joseph!" Pearl had walked to the end of the hall and was standing at the open door of the last room. Madrid and I walked over to him, and all three of us entered.

The sight was sickening.

A skeleton was sitting on the bed and leaning against the wall. As we got close to it, a bat flew out of its skull, causing us all to jump back.

The ghoulish scene caused both Madrid and me to stay where we were. This reluctance was not shared by Pearl, who walked right over to the skeleton and waved his arms to frighten the bat away. It flew around the room for a few seconds before exiting through a large hole in the ceiling.

Pearl grabbed the skeleton by the arm as if he planned to shake hands with it. I expected the arm or the hand to crumble and fall off at his touch, but it remained intact. Then he pulled the skeleton toward him and examined the back of the skull.

"Like I thought," he said, pointing to a tag on the back. "Made in China."

Madrid and I both exhaled at the same time.

"This guy is seriously screwed up," said Pearl. "It's a skeleton like medical schools use to teach with."

"He set this all up for someone to find and be scared," I said. "It worked."

"It worked with me," said Pearl. "It scared me shitless for a minute." He looked at us. "But only for a minute."

"If Delgado can put things slightly off kilter, then he's happy," said Madrid. "He is beyond being merely nuts. He's a psychopath. I'm afraid Maxine March is in serious danger."

"If he hasn't bumped her off by now or caused her to die of fright," muttered Pearl.

Madrid glared at the big detective, I suppose in deference to my feelings.

"I was only sayin' what we all were thinkin'," he said. "I am what I am and being subtle is not included in my makeup. Sorry if I offended you for tellin' the truth. I've been around this kind of shit all my life. When you're a cop in a big city, you see it all. I guess I got callous a long time ago. But facts is facts. This gal may be a goner."

Madrid started to admonish his investigator again, but I put up my hand. "It's okay, Lorenzo. He's probably right. I do need to face the fact that Delgado might have already killed her, even in the past few days. He may just be playing with us. But we've got to at least try to find out what happened to her. I can't stand not knowing."

"More important for you, Tom, is the need to find out about her so we can clear you once and for all," said the attorney. "I care about that above all else."

"What do we do?" I asked. "We know she was here by what Maria told me. That's all we've got."

"We can start by looking around in this loony bin," said Pearl.

"I wish you wouldn't keep saying that," I said. "People with mental problems are sick. They have enough trouble without being made fun of!"

"It is what it is," he said. "I think it was you who said that this guy Delgado is nuts. What's the difference between calling someone 'nuts' and calling this place a 'loony bin'? I have ta tell ya, I don't see it." Pearl shrugged his shoulders and walked out in the hall.

Madrid walked over to me and whispered, "Ray's a bit rough around the edges, but he's really good. You'll be glad he's on our team."

"Yeah, I guess."

"He's crass," said Madrid, "but the world he and I deal with—and that you have been thrust into dealing with—is not one that worries much about niceties. You're used to the academic world where the weapons are primarily words, not actions."

"Yeah, you're right. The daggers you get in your back are literal, not figurative. But it seems like Delgado has gone over into your world."

"Not much more to see in here," he said. "Let's check out the other rooms on this floor."

The two of us walked out into the hall and split up. We could hear Pearl banging around at the other end, so we picked the rooms near to where we were standing.

I walked into the room next to the one we had just exited. It was similar to the other one: a metal framed bed was against the wall to the left, a chest of drawers to the right, a single chair by the window, and a free-standing cabinet for clothes. A small door at the end opened into a tiny bathroom containing a toilet and a wash basin. It smelled so bad that I gagged and slammed the door. This place was really disgusting now, but I imagine it was not this bad in its heyday. Patients probably lived quite differently, even though they weren't free to leave.

Blankets and sheets had been taken off the bed, revealing a mattress that was stained over its entire surface. Under the bed, I found something that I first thought was a bathrobe. I reached under and dragged it out—I was sorry I did. It was a frayed straitjacket with large spots of blood showing. I quickly threw it down.

Absent mindedly, I pulled the bed out from the wall. At the point where the wall joined the floor, I noticed that the baseboard was loose, as if it had been pulled out and pushed back.

I bent down and probed the wall. At first, the old plaster wall seemed solid, then I found a hole. I yanked on the baseboard and it came away from the wall all along this side of the room. Now I could see the hole, which looked to be the size of my hand.

I reached in and ran my hand to the left, finding nothing. When I moved it to the right, however, my fingers grazed across an object. At first, I could not quite grasp it. I did not want to push it farther along and out of reach, so I moved my fingers carefully around and soon encountered what felt like a strap. I tugged on that and could feel the object moving. I pulled it toward the small opening and it caught. I reached in and discovered that it had an oblong shape. I moved it so the narrower end was facing the hole, and it easily slid out.

As I picked up my prize, I knew instantly what it was. I was holding Maxine's Leica camera.

June 27, 2005

On the drive back to the valley the day before, we had all agreed that the film in Maxine's camera might hold the answers about what had happened to her. I was heartened about any sign that she could still be alive, although the photos might yield nothing.

The camera was also a direct link to her. I knew how much she treasured it—her father had given it to her many years ago, and she rarely let it out of her sight. She disdained the newer digital models because she felt that film cameras offered more potential to produce true art. Digital cameras made it too easy. "All artists must suffer," she had said to me with a laugh.

She had only let me see a few of her photos once, and I found them very good. Many looked European in their starkness and occasional odd subject matter, like the French master Henri Cartier-Bresson.

"You're a writer, not a photographer," she said, when she put them away after allowing me to look at them only briefly.

"But I've worked with photographers for years and on many assignments," I had protested. "I know good shots when I see them."

"You're a writer," she repeated, and that was that. I did not protest, but hated to be dismissed so abruptly.

I was thinking about Maxine and her camera now, as I drove to Salem to meet Madrid and Pearl. I had given the camera to Madrid the day before on our drive back to civilization. He planned to ask a friend who worked in a photo lab to get the shots developed quickly. We had agreed to meet in his office at noon today to look over the photos.

Madrid must have been watching for me out the window because he met me in his outer office and led me back to a conference room. Pearl was already there.

"So, what do we have?" I asked.

"A real mixed bag," said Pearl, who had been looking at the photos with a magnifying glass when I walked in. He pushed the stack of them over to me as I sat down.

Maxine's photos included ones she had taken around Corvallis and on campus—of lovers strolling hand in hand by the river, a little boy flying a kite on the beach, a covered bridge, an old woman rummaging through a garbage can, two old men sitting on a park bench feeding the birds, and a nude woman on the back of an elephant. Typical subjects of Maxine's.

"Jesus," said Pearl, pointing to the elephant shot, "what does *that* mean? Was she seeing a shrink?"

"You're in there too, Tom," said Madrid, as I reached the shots he was talking about.

I vaguely remembered that Maxine had been taking pictures of us at our picnic in McDonald Forest. That was just before we heard the explosion and found the body of Madrid's former client, Hector Morales. It was also the last time I saw her.

She had taken a few shots of me clowning around and one in a time-lapse mode of the two of us sitting on a log. It was after that that I kissed her for the first time. I turned away so the two of them could not see how this made me feel.

"Keep going, Tom. There's more that is pertinent to our case," said Madrid.

I cleared my throat. "Sure, yeah, I will."

In the next few shots, Maxine seemed to be trying to record where she was. As a photographer, I guess she felt more comfortable leaving visual clues than the written ones I would have used.

There was a shot of what looked like one of the rooms in the Animal Isolation Lab, where I had just been. It showed the primitive cot I had seen, the dirt floor, a small wooden table and chair, and a tin plate and cup.

"It's like Devil's Island," I muttered. "A real hellhole."

I picked up the magnifying glass and studied the photo more closely. "Look at this," I said. "Isn't this a date scrawled in the dirt on the floor?"

Pearl grabbed the photo. "It sure as hell is—6/15/05. She's tellin' us when she was there. Not bad, for an amateur."

"Let's see," said Madrid. He looked at the tiny numbers through the magnifying glass. "That's exactly what she was doing. She did not feel able to get out of there, maybe did not know where she was, but hoped someone would find the camera and develop the film eventually."

"God," I said, "why is he putting her through this?"

"Obviously, he's afraid she will tell what she knows about him," said Madrid. "But I guess he cares enough about her from their past association that he can't bring himself to kill her, like he has everyone else who has gotten in his way."

"At least not yet," said Pearl, ever the blunt realist.

I gulped at that statement, although I knew he was right. Delgado was ruthless enough to do anything.

"So, he grabbed her and locked her up in this lab and then moved her to the sanitarium," said Pearl.

"And she took photos along the way to leave a trail she hoped someone would find," added Madrid. "Maybe you, Tom?"

"Maybe so. At least I hope so."

"I don't get how she could take the photos with him not seein' her," continued Pearl. "I mean, he's no dummy."

"I think I know," I said. "She once showed me how she got some of these more sensational shots. She never asked permission to take a photo, and the things she recorded people doing were not always flattering. She would hide the camera in her clothing or her purse and she was good at it. My guess is she did the same thing here. Probably Delgado didn't search her, so she got away with it."

"Keep goin'," said Pearl, impatiently. "There's more."

Next, Maxine had taken shots of the sanitarium that were of exhibit quality. Wonderful views of the exterior of the building from unusual angles, plus shots of the interior that told a story even without captions. The long halls leading to rooms where people lived who were there for a cure from the healing waters. The bleak rooms themselves with their Spartan bed, dresser, chair combinations. Scraps of photos and letters and postcards like the one I found. The sign in the tub room about the cures that were possible. And then the tubs themselves, with the slings suspended over them to drop the sufferers into the boiling cauldrons until they convulsed and were dragged across the room to the beds for recovery— or not. There was even a photo of a typical group shot of doctors, nurses, and patients lined up in front of the main building, circa 1937.

I guess Delgado must have allowed her to roam around the old building, making sure she did not try to get away. Neither he nor she was pictured, but I was certain he was always nearby. His mercurial manner probably made her wonder if he would let her go after giving her a good scare about keeping his secrets. But that was not to be as revealed in the last series of photos: Maxine in the room where I found the camera. In another time-lapse shot, there she was, looking unsmilingly and directly into the camera with sad eyes and holding up a finger with blood on the tip. The next frame showed a wall with *6/16/05* written on it, presumably in blood.

"That was the day after she was in the basement of the lab— the date I saw scrawled in the dust," I said. "I didn't see anything like that on the wall."

Madrid picked up the photo and studied it carefully. "Maybe he was getting ready to move her," he said, "so she had to get rid of it. Taking those photos was a pretty gutsy thing to do."

"And pretty desperate," I said. "I wonder why she didn't just leave the film and take the camera."

"Hard to say," said Pearl. "Desperate people do odd things. She seems to have had a reason for everything else, so maybe there's a reason for this, too."

"When we find her, we'll ask her," said Madrid, smiling at me reassuringly.

"So, where does this leave us?" I asked. "What do we do to find her?"

"Wait a minute," said Pearl. "There's one last photo you gotta see. You won't even believe it!" He handed the last picture to me. It showed Maxine standing on a chair and hugging a moose. "Now that is fuckin' unbelievable," said Pearl, shaking his head. "It's worse than the one with a naked gal on the elephant. What is it with this woman and animals!"

I smiled and sat back in my chair, holding the photo up to the light for a better look. "Strange as it may seem, I am very familiar with him. Let me tell you about Mr. Moose." And I did—the whole strange tale that was now crystal clear to me.

"So, Delgado stole the moose from the museum and pulled the stuffing out and then filled it with the cocaine he was smuggling in to pay for his renegade research into Ebola fever?" asked Madrid, shaking his head in disbelief.

"That's the way it looks," I said.

"You shoulda tole us," said Pearl. "We need to know this stuff."

"I didn't see any link between my case and the missing moose," I said. "I was just looking for it as a favor for one of my bosses at the university. Until I found the stuffing and the cocaine in the basement of the lab, I didn't see any link at all. And then I didn't mention it because we got all caught up in going to the sanitarium, and it slipped my mind. I am sorry. I should have said something sooner."

"It doesn't matter at this point," said Madrid to Pearl. "What matters is how do we find Maxine March?"

* * * * *

I drove directly to my house in Newport that afternoon. I needed to get away from town so I could think—about my fractious life, crumbling career, and finding Maxine.

As I walked in the door, I saw that the message light was blinking on my answer machine. I picked it up to find one message.

"Professor Martindale, this is Pat Thompson in Lincoln City. We talked last week about my painting of that old hospital in the Coast Range. I need to talk to you. Please call me."

I dialed her number and waited on the line.

"Hello."

"Pat? Hi. It's Tom Martindale. I was calling . . ."

"This isn't Pat. It's her daughter, Sarah."

"Oh, yes, hello. Is your mother there?"

"No, she isn't. Are you the writer she called about her painting of that spooky old hospital up in the mountains?"

"Yeah, that's me."

"She told me all about that old place and the painting she did of it."

"A great painting," I said. "I really like it."

"Are you interested in it to buy?"

Sarah Thompson was sounding a bit suspicious, but I was not about to get into the whole story. I didn't have the time, and she didn't need to know anything more than what her mother had already told her.

"No, I just saw it in the window of a gallery and wanted to know where she found the building. That's all."

"Well, you got my mother into her amateur detective mode, and she's been obsessed with that place ever since you met with her. She doesn't talk about anything else now, and she's determined to figure out why you wanted to know about that place. I guess you didn't tell her much."

"No, I didn't. There wasn't much to tell." Not to a nosy old woman, I thought to myself, rather unkindly.

"Well, she didn't believe that."

I was getting impatient. "Please just tell her I called."

"The thing is, I think she's gone out to that place, and I'm worried about her," said Sarah. "She left yesterday and didn't come back last night. That's not like my mom."

"She went out there alone?" I asked. "I thought she always traveled around with a nature group or something."

"You don't know my mom. When she gets an idea into her head, there's no stopping her. Whatever it is you told her really got her juices flowing. She's not all that young any more, Mr. Martindale. She could be in real trouble."

"Have you called the police?"

"No, I haven't. I just got here from Portland. I drove over when I couldn't reach her on the phone. But I don't think I should call the police. I think it is your responsibility to go up to that place and find her. She's only in this mess because of you!"

Sarah Thompson was as direct as her mother, and she had a point. But how was I to know that Pat would put herself in danger because of her suspicions about what I was looking into?"

"Are you still on the line?" said the daughter.

"Yeah, I'm here. I was thinking. You're right. I owe it to your mom to try to figure this out. Are you going to stay over here for a while?"

"Yes, until I find my mother."

"Okay, good. I'll be back in touch."

Even though it was late in the afternoon, I grabbed a coat and a flashlight and was out the door in five minutes.

By driving to the town of Logsden, I was hoping to get to the sanitarium more quickly than if I had gone around and come in from the other side, as I had with Madrid and Pearl. Lorenzo had given me a copy of the forest service map he had used the day before. It now helped me navigate the tangle of logging roads that would get me to the hospital.

I was very leery of driving on these primitive roads. I had once gotten lost farther south in the Coast Range and, when I didn't see that a road had been washed out, my car slipped over a high cliff. I leaped to safety just in time. I had a better car now, an SUV equipped with four-wheel drive.

The roads were narrow but dry, so I created a cloud of dust with every mile I drove. That worked to my benefit at the three places I encountered log trucks that were heading out with full loads. Once, I saw a truck coming and was able to pull out in a wider spot. Another time, one of the big rigs stopped up a hill to let me pass. I was surprised that they were working this late in the day.

Before long, I was above the tree line and stopped to get my bearings. To the west, I could see the ocean glistening in the distance. According to the map, I was near Fanno Peak, elevation 3,333. I could see it in the distance, and it still had some snow on it even now, in the summer.

I drove on and came to the same kind of washed out road I had encountered in this mountain range before. The winters were brutal and the roads were not all that good to begin with. I pulled over to the side of the road and got out of my car. I was on a high ridge with a valley below me. Through my binoculars, I could see the sanitarium. I was on the opposite side from where we had arrived before, but this was the closest I could get by vehicle. I would still have to hike down and then up again. It was now nearly 7 P.M. and it would be dark when I got to my destination. I headed out, tying the sleeves of my jacket around my waist in case it got chilly later on.

At first, my walk was unobstructed. The path down the hill was clear of brush as if it had been trimmed on purpose. When I reached the bottom, however, the going got rougher. The ground became mushy and oozy and hard to walk on. In fact, like before, my shoes disappeared in the muck with the first step I took and one even came off. I reached down and pulled both shoes off, as well as my now filthy socks. I slogged on.

At a point near the bottom, a sound to my left caused me to stop. I felt very vulnerable out in the middle of this open area, with little protection except for the brush. I listened.

Soon, a huge elk leaped out of the trees and ran right in front of me. I was so startled I almost didn't see that two more were following close behind. I waited for them to disappear into the trees to my right before resuming my trek.

As it always seemed to happen when I am out in the wilderness, I was soon disheveled and miserable. My clothes were dirty, my shoes were muddy, and I wanted only to go home.

I stopped to rest on a large boulder when I got to the other side of the cleared area. It was now almost 8 P.M., and the sun had dropped below the ridge I had just descended. Even though it was summer, the air was turning cold. I put on my jacket and fished some clean socks out of the pocket. I put them on and then donned my mushy shoes.

I was ready to make the climb up to the sanitarium, which was above me on the ridge. I could see its menacing outline in the gathering dusk. As I got close to the top, I heard loud talking and laughter. I stopped and listened. Music also wafted through the air—Mexican music.

I moved off the path to my left and stopped on a ledge that was wide enough to stand on—if I was careful. I lifted my head to a point that was even with the edge of the ground and looked over. I was about fifty yards away from the north end of the building, an area where a large terrace extended out.

A group of men were sitting around a fire, eating and drinking and looking very relaxed. At the far end, a man in a white apron was standing over a barbecue pit, smoke pouring out of whatever he was cooking on the spit. The music was blaring from a radio resting on a log near where he was working.

As I looked closer, I saw that the men had guns near them—on the ground or in their waistbands. Within a few minutes, however, this bucolic scene was shattered by the sound of a powerful truck, which roared into the area and lurched to a halt, barely missing the fire pit. All the men stood up quickly, some dropping their plates in the process. They all picked up their guns and seemed to be snapping to attention in a military manner.

The occupants of the truck did not get out immediately. Apparently for effect, they were sitting inside and watching the others. In a few minutes, however, the door on the passenger side opened and a boot touched the ground. It looked expensive and was highly polished. The toe was covered in silver. The other boot joined its counterpart on the ground, and a man emerged.

He was well over six feet tall and was wearing a leather jacket to match his leather pants. He glanced around the group, but I couldn't tell where he was looking because he was wearing sunglasses, despite the absence of sunshine.

"Lobo," he said loudly.

The group took a collective breath as one of the largest dogs I have ever seen jumped down from the rear of the truck. He stood by his master and sniffed the air. My mouth went dry as I ducked my head below the surface of the ridge.

ven though I have always loved dogs—and they, me—I had no intention of getting anywhere near this monster. For one thing, he looked like he was part wolf. For another, he had probably been trained to kill on command.

I started backing away from the top of the ridge and partway down the trail. When I was about fifty yards away, I turned around and walked as fast as I could into the forest. As I did so, a shiver or two went up and down my spine. I broke into a run once I reached the trees and continued until I felt I was out of sniffing range of the dog.

What to do? If Pat Thompson had made it to the sanitarium, she was probably being held by these guys or, sad to even think it, dead. I owed it to her to find out. I was also very curious about this gang. They were obviously part of the Mexican drug gang, probably contacted by Delgado to smuggle the cocaine. This remote place was ideal for that kind of transaction.

I circled around to the east and walked until I could see the front of the building. The slight breeze was blowing away from me toward the west. I hoped that the dog would not pick up my scent as I moved in closer. I paused each time I moved forward to listen. No growls from the dog or yells from the men, just the music. Surprisingly, there were no guards posted on the perimeter of the property.

I moved around to the other end of the building, opposite where the men were standing, and spied a ground-level door I had not seen before. On my previous visits, I had gone in and out of the door to the rear that led to the kitchen. I held my breath, counted to ten and ran across the yard to the end door.

I looked through the broken glass in the door and saw that the hall ahead of me was clear. I grabbed the door knob and pushed gently. Although it was locked, the hinges were so rusted they gave way to the slight pressure I put on the door.

I closed the door carefully and stepped into the room to the left, so no one would see me standing in the hall. Like all the rooms, it was full of debris and the sad memories of the people who had lived in it over the years. A faded and tattered calendar for the year 1939 hung on the far wall. A yellowing photo of a young boy and girl standing by a carousel was stuck in the mirror atop the dresser.

In my search for Pat, I went from room to room, worrying all the time that one of the men would see me through the window. She was not in any of the first floor rooms, so I climbed the stairs. I peeked around the corner before stepping into the upper hall. A man was sitting on a chair about halfway down. He was smoking a cigarette and leaning back in his chair with his feet on an old trunk, seemingly daydreaming as he blew smoke rings up toward the high ceiling.

With his back to me, I was able to dart into the first room in that section of the building. In the fading light of day, I could see that it was filled with old furniture and piles of books and files, many of them damaged by water that had dripped down over the years from a corroded pipe in the ceiling.

Luckily, this room was connected to the one next to it by a small bathroom that had served both rooms. I walked through the filthy bathroom and stepped into an equally damaged and depressing space. I was now just one room away from where the guard was sitting. The hall door was open, and I glanced out at him. He had finished his cigarette and was now turning the pages of a magazine, smiling and smacking his lips at the big breasted women looking seductively back at him.

"Jaime!"

I froze at the sound of a voice from below.

"*Andale, andale!*"

The man got up and walked quickly past the room I was in, to the end of the hall.

"*Si*, Pedro."

"Get your skinny ass down here, *mi amigo*. It is time to eat!"

"*Si.*"

With no hesitation, the man walked down the stairs, his boots thudding hard against each step. I waited for several minutes before stepping out into the hall. Then I quickly walked to the room he had been guarding. There, tied to a chair with a gag in her mouth, was Pat Thompson.

I put a finger to my lips and knelt down to remove the gag and untie her.

"Pat, God I'm glad to see you! Are you okay?"

As soon as her hands were free, she hugged me for a long time. "Tom, I had given up hope of anyone ever finding me in this place! How did you . . ."

"I'll explain later, but we've got to get out of here before Jaime comes back and finds us. I think he's eating, so we've got maybe fifteen minutes." I untied her feet and helped her up. "Can you walk?"

She began massaging her legs. "I'm okay. I'm in pretty good shape for an old lady," she smiled.

I led her quickly out into the hall, and we started down the stairs.

"Wait!" she whispered.

"There's no time!"

"It will only take a minute."

She disappeared back down the hall. My stomach churned as I watched the hall below, expecting Jaime and the others to appear at any time.

Pat was back in a few seconds. "I couldn't leave these behind." In her hands, she was carrying a sketchbook and a camera.

"There's a small door at the end of the lower hall," I whispered. "We'll go out that way."

We were poised to walk through it, when I saw one of the men coming around the end of the building, leading the dog on a leash. I pushed Pat into a room to the side and closed the door, praying that the man would not walk in and the dog would not smell us.

We waited for five minutes before I dared chance another look outside. It seemed all clear, so I opened the door and pointed to the trees across the yard.

"Go as fast as you can!"

"What you mean is that I should run like hell!" she whispered.

"Do it now!"

And we did just that, with Pat in the lead and me following close behind. As we ran, I expected that bullets would be whizzing past us at any moment, or that the huge wolf dog would overtake and attack us. Neither happened, and we reached the forest unscathed.

As we stopped to rest under the cover of trees, I saw the dog without his leash watching us from the front of the building. None of the men were in sight, but he had definitely seen us.

"Start walking slowly into the forest," I whispered. "Don't make any sudden movements." Pat did what I said.

The dog seemed transfixed by the sight of us and did not move or bark. I held my breath. The dog started walking toward us as if he wanted a closer look. He stopped about halfway across the field. My heart was beating fast because I knew we could not outrun him. Maybe I could distract him while Pat climbed a tree.

I moved backward at a glacial pace, keeping my eyes on the dog. By this time, Pat had reached the dense forest, and I was nearly there myself. Just as I reached the safety of the forest, the man who had been walking Lobo before walked around the building carrying a dish. The man followed the dog's line of sight and got out his binoculars. I held my breath. I was certain we were far enough back to be hidden in the trees, but I did not want to take any chances.

The man spoke to the dog, saying what sounded like *"Loco* Lobo." Then he put the dish down. The dog started eating and the man moved away.

We got out of there as fast as we could.

* * * * *

Pat had parked her car in Valsetz on the other side of the sanitarium. Getting there required that we drive a long way. But it did give us time to talk.

"Do you always take chances like that?" I asked.

"What do you think, Tom? I'm seventy-five years old. I was only getting a closer look at that place to improve my painting."

"I don't believe that for a minute," I said. "Your painting is finished and up for sale in a gallery. You were trying to find out why I was so curious about what you painted, admit it."

She smiled and drank from the bottle of water we were sharing. "I'll take the Fifth on that."

"You do something like that again, and you'll need to drink a fifth of something stronger than water to quiet your nerves. Do you have any idea what those guys would have done to you?"

She laughed heartily. "I'm too old to be put into a white slavery ring," she said with a grin. Pat had a great sense of humor, even when it came to something this serious. "Are you ever going to tell me what this is all about?" she asked. "After all of this, I think I've earned the right to know."

She had a point.

"I'll tell you what you want to know if you promise to stay away from that place."

"Okay, I promise. I'll stick to seascapes."

We were now back to civilization and on paved roads. We turned north at the junction with Highway 229 at Siletz.

"I have reason to believe that the woman I was accused of killing, Maxine March, had been held in that place."

"Poor woman," said Pat. "Did she escape? I didn't see anyone else there."

"She didn't escape, but was probably taken some place else before you got there."

"Who was holding her?"

"Her ex-husband, Duncan Delgado. I think he set me up for killing her."

"And she's not dead."

"No, at least as of a few days ago, but I need to prove it so I can get off the hook with the authorities. It's as simple as that, but it's also real complicated. She has disappeared, and so has he."

"I think maybe he was at the sanitarium," she said.

I nearly drove the car off the narrow road. "You saw Duncan Delgado?"

"I think so."

"When?"

"When I first got there yesterday afternoon," she said. "You know, I've only been gone a day. It's not like I was lost."

"Yeah, yeah, yeah! Go on."

"I was up in the room where you found me, shooting items I might paint later—iron beds, chairs, broken windows. I heard a sound behind me, and when I looked around, this dashing-looking man was standing there, smiling at me."

"What did he say?"

"He asked me what I was doing there. I said I was a painter, and I was just making sketches to use later, after I got back home. I had hidden my camera in my backpack, but showed him my sketch pad."

"He believed you?"

"I guess so. He glanced at the pages and handed them back. He told me I had better leave for my own safety. He said this was a dangerous place with lots of hazards."

"And what did you do?"

"I obeyed his orders. I was beginning to feel a bit funny about all of this and thought it best to get out of there."

"And he was going to let you go? I can't believe that!"

"Look at it from his perspective. He finds this harmless old woman in this rundown hospital who reminds him of his mother and . . ."

"If he ever had a mother!" I snapped.

"Whatever, but I think he sized me up as that kind of harmless person and decided to let me go. He helped me gather up my stuff and held my arm as we walked down the stairs. He even said he would drive me to my car."

"But he changed his mind."

"No, the other men changed it for him. Before we could leave the area, some trucks carrying those Mexican gentlemen drove in, and we were both surrounded in seconds. Delgado argued with one man who seemed to be the leader for a time, and then two of the other men took me by the arms back up to the room where you found me."

"They tied you up?"

"Not at first. They motioned for me to sit on the bed and then they left the room. They closed the door, but did not even lock it."

"And what did you do?"

"I got out my camera and started shooting pictures out of the window. They were all standing right below me, so I had a clear view. There was something pretty peculiar going on besides the men talking and milling around. I even saw a . . ."

"You took photos of Delgado and the others?"

"Of course. They're all in here." She held up the preview screen of the camera. "It's all digital. Want to see?"

I pulled the car over to the side of the road when it was wide enough to do so safely. I turned off the ignition, and Pat handed me her camera.

"What do I press?"

"I thought college professors knew everything," she said.

"Don't tell anyone," I said. "They just think they do."

"If you keep pushing this button, the frames will advance."

As I did that, the photos of the view below Pat's vantage point appeared as if in a movie: Delgado walks out of the building and is surrounded by six men, all carrying rifles. He heads for one of the vehicles, a black Chevrolet Suburban, and stands by the open rear door. A frame or two later, he steps back to make way for the big man in the silver tipped boots I saw earlier.

They talk for a frame or two and, at one point, Delgado points to the building. He seems to be arguing with the big man. The others stand around with their hands on their weapons. Then, the man seems to be ordering Delgado to do something because he gets right up into his face and then pushes his shoulder. Delgado disappears from the screen.

"Did he leave?" I ask Pat.

"Just wait a minute, Tom, and you'll see what happened next. It's the strangest thing I have ever seen."

I pushed the button and soon saw what Pat meant. In a short time, Delgado comes back into view, pulling something on a rope. The tip of the object comes into view and then the object itself. Delgado has brought his *compadres* in crime a large moose.

h, yes. Mr. Moose," I said, as I handed Pat's camera back to her.

"You know about this moose?" she said, a startled look on her face.

"Yes, it's been missing from the university museum for a few weeks. Some friends asked me to find it."

Pat started laughing. "So, in addition to finding a murderer and clearing your name and finding your friend, you are hunting for a lost moose."

"A lost *stuffed* moose," I said.

"I didn't think it was alive," she chortled. "It was not moving under its own power—it was on a platform with wheels."

At that statement, we both broke into one of those "laughed until I cried" moments. The whole thing sounded ridiculous. In fact, it *was* very ridiculous, and I marveled at how I had gotten involved in any of it in the first place.

"Please explain this, Tom," she said, as she started coughing. "Excuse me, I got choked on my own laughter."

"I thought you'd never ask," I said, getting into the spirit of her jocularity. "The moose was stolen from the museum about a month ago, as I said. I found evidence a few days ago that it might have been used as a way to transport cocaine into the state. I think that all or part of the straw stuffing was removed and replaced with bags of cocaine. The moose you saw was probably filled with the stuff and that is what Delgado was arguing about with Mr. Silver Toes. Any more shots? I don't see any more photos of the moose."

"There aren't any," she said. "About that time, I heard a noise in the hall, so I moved away from the window and sat down on the bed. I slipped the camera out of sight under the covers. Right after that, one of the men who had taken me up there came in with some food and water. I ate the food and drank some water, and then he tied me up. At that point, he did not put the gag in my mouth, however."

"What happened after that?"

"Before long, the boss came in for a chat."

"Did he hurt you? Torture you?"

"Oh, no, nothing like that. He was very polite, but we had trouble communicating because he spoke little English. He asked if I worked for Delgado, then he asked if I was Delgado's mother."

"Sounds like he could not figure you out."

"I think that's true. I don't look like I would ever be involved in anything illegal, let alone drug running."

"You could make a fortune," I laughed. "The granny drug smuggler. Who would suspect? You know, older people have been caught doing just that. Are you sure you aren't secretly working for the Mexican drug cartels?"

"I haven't done that in years," she said with a straight face. "Not since I retired."

"So, he believed you?"

"I guess so, because he left pretty quickly. I'm sure, though, that he didn't know what to do with me. His instincts as a killer told him to get rid of me. But he was also someone who maybe had a mother or a grandmother he loved. So he was torn about the whole thing."

"Did you see Delgado again?"

"No. I guess he left right after he got the moose out of storage. The man who was guarding me came in and checked the cords around my wrists and ankles and put the gag in my mouth."

I started the car and pulled back onto the road. We were now heading up Highway 101 and driving through Lincoln City, the town where Pat lived.

"Pat, you know it just occurred to me that I should drop you off at your house and pick up your car myself. After what you've been through, I think home is the best place for you. Can you do without your car for a day or so?"

"You bet I can," she said. "I was thinking the same thing myself. This has been quite a day. I think I need a good night's sleep and a big glass of wine, not necessarily in that order."

I turned onto the street that led into Roads End, the part of town where she lived. We drove in silence for a few minutes, until I pulled into her driveway.

"Did you give anyone your name during all of this?"

"No, oddly enough, no one asked or even looked at my driver's license. I guess they had bigger things on their minds—like a moose!"

"You got *that* right, I said. I don't think you have to worry about anyone coming for you here. But maybe you should leave town for a while, just in case."

"I have a condo in Portland," she said. "Maybe I will go up there for a week or so, just in case, and take my daughter with me. But I'll need my car to do that." She handed me the keys. "It's a Lexus. You can't miss it."

"I'll either go get it or make sure someone I trust gets it and has it to you by tomorrow," I said.

"That will be fine. In the meantime, what are you going to do?"

"First, I'm going to get these photos of yours processed and have prints made. Can I borrow your camera? I'll be careful with it."

"Of course," she said, as she handed it to me. "Don't delete the other images you'll find in there. I did shoot some parts of that creepy place and some objects I may want to paint."

"I will make sure that those frames are protected."

She opened the door. "I'll bet you're also going to go searching for that moose and for Duncan Delgado."

"You guessed right on both counts. Pat, you are a real trooper. I admire you very much, and I'm sorry if I got you into this mess. I didn't mean for you to put yourself in danger."

"That part is not your fault, Tom. I did it to myself. Please keep me posted on all of this. I promise not to pester you anymore. My days as an amateur sleuth are over."

"Glad to hear it."

I waited until she was safely opening the front door of her house and returned her wave as I drove away.

ven though it was 10 P.M., I headed right for Salem and called Lorenzo Madrid along the way to tell him when I would be at his office. He was waiting for me in the reception room.

"Tom, good to see you. Come on back."

He pointed to a chair and sat down behind his desk. I was glad that Raymond Pearl was not there. Although I knew Madrid trusted him, I had never felt entirely comfortable with him.

He poured us both a cup of coffee.

"Before we talk about what I've got, I wanted to ask you about Maria and her son. Are they all right?"

"Yes, they are fine. Treena moved them to a shelter in Portland where they will be safe until I figure out how to get Maria some kind of temporary status with the Immigration Service. It won't be easy, but I have some ideas that have worked in special cases like this in the past."

"That's great. I have been worried about her."

"So, what do you have?"

I pulled Pat's camera out of my briefcase and handed it to him. Unlike me, he knew exactly how to view the images.

I told him what had happened to Pat, and how I had gone to find her.

"You just keep getting yourself into tight spot after tight spot," he said, shaking his head in disbelief. "Do you have a death wish, Tom?"

I ignored his admonition.

"What am I looking for here?" he asked.

"What you have there is proof that Duncan Delgado is in the area and that he used the moose to transport cocaine," I said.

Madrid whistled. "*Carumba! Dios mio!* This is something! But we don't actually see the cocaine in the moose. Is this all the shots she took?"

"The men who were holding her came back and tied her up. She was careful to hide the camera, and for some reason they didn't search her."

"Mexicans respect their elders," he said. "So, what do you think—did Delgado get the moose and fill it with cocaine he got from someone in Mexico and then turn it all over to these guys? Or did they have the cocaine already and then he got the moose as a new kind of transport?"

"I think the first scenario is the correct one," I said. "He got the cocaine and sold it to them, moose and all. He'll use the money to continue his research into Ebola."

"It's all so convoluted," said Madrid, "like the Iran-Contra scandal of the 1980s, where the U. S. government sold arms to Iran and used the money to fund the guerilla war against the government of Nicaragua. So preposterous that it actually worked—for a while."

"Until they got caught," I said. "It sounds exactly like that, you're right. So, what do we do?"

"I think we call in the state police or the DEA. You agree?"

"Yeah, it's bigger than we are, certainly. But I'd like to call my friend Paul Bickford first—if I can reach him. He's the one who tipped me off about the sanitarium in the first place. He may know all about this already. I'd like to try to find out more from him before we talk to anyone here."

"You know, Tom, as an officer of the court, I am duly bound to report all suspicious activity I encounter in the course of practicing law," said Madrid.

"Can you give me until tomorrow to talk to Paul?"

Madrid thought for a moment before he answered. "Okay, I agree, as long as you promise to stay far away from Ocean Springs Sanitarium."

"I promise. I'm driving straight home to Corvallis. But what about picking up Pat Thompson's car in Valsetz?"

"I'll send Ray Pearl and one of the boys who helps me around here with odd jobs. I trust them both."

"Okay. Sounds good to me. Here are the keys and the directions to her house in Lincoln City. I promised to have the car back to her tomorrow."

"That will not be a problem, my friend. Let me know what you find out from Paul Bickford, and then we will figure out where to go from there."

"Oh, and will you burn me a CD of those photos? I may want to send them to Bickford."

In a few seconds, Madrid had done that and handed me the CD. I stood up, and we shook hands. I left his office thinking that for just this once, I would do what I said I would do. No more cockamamie schemes—at least for now.

June 28, 2005

I n the all the years I had known Paul Bickford, he had always appeared and disappeared from my life at various times as if he were a puff of smoke on the wind.

That was the case now. After tipping me off about the sanitarium and the possibility that Maxine March was still alive, he had vanished. The more I delved into the mess I was in, the more vital it had become for me to talk to him.

Early the next morning, I tried one of the three numbers I had for him and crossed my fingers.

"Northern Arctic Trading Company." A new company name he was apparently using as a front.

"Mr. Bickford, please."

"There is no one here by that name, sir. Are you sure you have the right number?" The woman had a pleasant voice with a slight Southern accent.

"Yes, I am sure. If a man by the name of Paul Bickford were to come there or call in, would you tell him that Tom Martindale called to say hello?"

A slight chuckle. "Yes, sir, I could do just that for y'all. But I doubt that will happen."

"I thank you very much, ma'am."

Southern voices always bring out my chivalrous side. I hung up and started to look for the next of Bickford's numbers on my list. My phone rang.

"Hello, Tom. It's Paul. Are you alone?"

"Yes, I am. You made a speedy drop-in to a place you have never been before. Remarkable."

"And may I congratulate you on uttering one of the most convoluted sentences of all time. 'If a man named Paul Bickford were to come there?' Jesus! I'll have to save it to give to your students at some point in the future. They won't believe it!"

"A convoluted sentence to track down a convoluted man," I said.

"I have to work hard at it," he laughed. "Enough of this prattle. How are you enjoying life outside the slammer?"

"Very much, and I thank you again for helping me get out."

"I don't know what you're talking about, Tom. I am not in the business of freeing felons."

"I'd ask you to cut out the bullshit, Paul, if I thought it would do any good."

"I won't take offense at that insult, professor, except to remind you that you give me too much credit for accomplishing things I have no control over," he continued. "So, what's on your mind?"

"I followed your lead and found that abandoned sanitarium in the Coast Range. I found some clues to make me believe that Maxine March is still alive."

"Go on."

"I also discovered that some Mexican bad guys may be using that place as a staging area for their drug smuggling."

"Go on."

"You don't seem at all surprised at what I've been telling you."

Bickford said nothing.

"I assume no answer means I'm correct."

More silence.

"Paul, did this connection go bad? Can you hear me now?"

"I'm here, Tom. I'm just waiting for you to finish your story."

"Okay, I'll do that. Duncan Delgado is involved in the smuggling. He has somehow gotten in touch with this gang and, I think, sold them cocaine. When it is sold, he will use the money to further fund his research into Ebola fever. You probably know all of this, but you may not know that the means of transporting the cocaine is fairly unique."

"And what might that be, Tom?"

"A moose."

"I beg your pardon. How can a moose be a means of transport for drugs? You must mean a mule or a team of mules, but usually that term is used to describe people who transport cocaine by swallowing balloons filled with the stuff."

I smiled to myself. Finally, I knew something Bickford did not. "You think it's impossible to hoist some saddlebags onto the back of a moose? I mean, you could train one to stand by a tall platform so you could reach the saddlebags."

"Tom, you are so full of shit on this. I think you've been ingesting some kind of illegal substance yourself. What the hell are you talking about?"

I laughed out loud. "I am savoring the moment, Paul. This is the first time I know something that you do not. I love the feeling of power."

"Well, don't let it go to your head, professor. It won't happen again. Now tell me what you're feeling so high and mighty about!"

"Delgado used an old stuffed moose he stole from the

university museum to transport the cocaine into the state."

"Now, *that* is a novel way to move drugs," he laughed. "I've heard of putting cocaine into everything from statues of the Madonna to Indian Kachina dolls, but never anything that large. That's like a Trojan horse!"

"He took the old straw stuffing out of the moose and filled it with cocaine," I said.

"It wouldn't have been the loose powder itself," continued Bickford. "It had to be in bricks of cocaine. That's how they package it, you know. Each brick is about the size of a Bible."

"I'm not sure of the particulars yet, but I've seen evidence that he had the moose and turned it over to some bad guys at the old sanitarium."

"What kind of evidence?"

"Photos of him with some Mexican drug smugglers and with the moose."

"How long ago?"

"Earlier today."

"Jesus! Can you get me those photos?"

"I can transmit them to you now. Give me an e-mail address."

He did that, and I inserted the disk and sent the photos. There was silence on the line as Bickford waited to get them. I could hear the hum of his computer.

"Shit. That looks like Jesus Maldanado. He's a big drug kingpin from Mexico, who usually operates in California. First time I knew he was working in Oregon. Must have been a big shipment for him to leave his home base in L.A."

"I guess a moose can hold a lot of kilos of anything—certainly of cocaine," I said.

"One thing these guys probably didn't know, though, is that early taxidermists like the one who prepared your moose used arsenic on the skin as an insecticide to keep their animal specimens from being damaged by bugs."

"That sounds lethal," I said.

"Maybe not," he said. "The cocaine is usually wrapped in neoprene, but sometimes the guys who package it get careless, and I guess some of it could leak out."

"Too bad if some druggy got sick," I said cynically.

"Yeah, I agree," he said. "But the arsenic is so old that any toxic effects are probably long gone. If it happened to mix with the cocaine, it would probably make it taste funny, but I doubt it would kill anybody."

"How do you know stuff like that, Paul?" I asked.

"I make it my business to know a lot of trivia, in case I need it," he laughed.

"Reporters do the same thing, although no one ever asks for it."

"You got that right. Tell me, Tom, how did you come by these photos?" asked Paul.

"It's a long story that we don't have time for now, but they are from a credible source. You can trust me on that."

"Okay, I believe you. I've got to move on this now, before all of this stuff gets dumped on the streets of cities in your fair state."

"I didn't realize that you got involved in this kind of thing, Paul. I thought you were Army Special Ops and worked mostly overseas."

"Let's just say that I am on a special detail now. I can't say any more."

"Can you help me find Delgado and, through him, Maxine March?"

"Ah, yes, your old lady love."

"That's not entirely the case, Paul. I want to find her to make sure she's safe, but I also need her to walk into court to prove that I did not kill her. My attorney used that argument and the judge bought it, but I'm still not off the hook."

Bickford grasped the bizarre details of my situation immediately.

"Now that is what I call a real conundrum," he laughed. "You know I'll do what I can for you. I think it's fair to say that you'll be seeing me very soon—I need to get out there and sort this all out. And we've got to stop these guys."

I exhaled loudly. "That's music to my ears. Thanks! I can really use your help, Paul."

"I need to debrief you and the person who took the photos. I'll be flying to Portland on a red-eye flight tonight and then I'll drive to Corvallis. You going to be home tomorrow morning?"

"I'll wait for your call. I'll be here. In the meantime, can you send me some material on the drug trade in Oregon? I'd like to know what we're dealing with here."

"Yeah, Tom. I'll have Candy send you what I've got."

"Candy. Somehow I knew that a sweet-sounding voice like hers would belong to a Candy."

"Don't mess with her, Tom. She knows karate."

*   *   *   *   *

Within a half hour, my fax machine came alive and I started receiving the background material Paul had promised to send on the drug scene in Oregon, especially cocaine smuggling.

FROM THE DRUG ENFORCEMENT
ADMINISTRATION

Drug Situation: Mexican drug trafficking organizations dominate the illicit drug market in Oregon. The state serves as a trans-shipment point for controlled substances smuggled from Mexico to Washington and Canada. Marijuana and MDMA (street name Ecstasy) from Canada also transit Oregon en route to other U. S. locations. While methamphetamine is a significant drug threat in Oregon, marijuana, heroin, cocaine, and club drugs are of concern. Drug trafficking organizations in Oregon also engage in

*money laundering, using a variety of methods to legitimize
and reposition illicit proceeds.*

*Cocaine: Cocaine is available throughout Oregon. While
the powder form is most prevalent, crack cocaine is found in
some urban areas. Mexican traffickers dominate wholesale
distribution, transporting the drug from Mexico, California,
and other southwestern states. Retail quantities are primarily sold by Mexican drug trafficking organizations, street
gangs, prison gangs, and local independent dealers.*

At various places in the report, Bickford had made notations.
"Interstate 5 is the main north/south corridor, but Highway 101
on the coast is closer to the forests these guys like to hide in," he
wrote at one point. "Meth is the biggest problem in your state,
but cocaine keeps rearing its ugly head, too."

FROM THE OFFICE OF NATIONAL
DRUG CONTROL POLICY

*. . . Oregon is ranked tenth in the nation for total land
area, with 97,060 square miles. The geography ranges from
coastal to high desert, separated by mountain ranges. The
state includes 2.5 million acres of forested land, 889 square
miles of inland water areas, and 296 miles of coastline.*

*. . . Identified drug trafficking organizations with links
to Mexico and Central America are responsible for the
majority of illegal methamphetamine, cocaine, heroin, and
marijuana imported into Oregon and have dominated the
illegal drug market. Recently, there has been an increase in
the smuggling of high-grade marijuana from British
Columbia (known as B.C. Bud) into and through Oregon.*

*The primary illegal drugs of abuse in order of usage are
marijuana, methamphetamine, heroin, and cocaine.
Oregon drug traffickers produce marijuana, methamphetamine, and psilocybin mushrooms for exportation to other*

areas of the country. *The Oregon geography provides con-
cealment for clandestine methamphetamine labs, smuggling activities, and marijuana growing operations.*

*The growing, importation, exportation, and manufacture
of illegal drugs in Oregon pose a significant threat to the
health and safety of Oregon communities, neighboring
states, and the rest of the nation . . .*

"Your state's got way too many remote areas to patrol
properly," Paul noted. "The bad guys always find the weakest link
in the chain and exploit it. The hills are alive with the sound of
music—and drug smugglers!"

FROM ATTORNEY GENERAL'S REPORT
"ORGANIZED CRIME IN OREGON"

*. . . Organized crime groups are insular in nature. The
leaders of these organizations know that law enforcement
agencies may seek to penetrate the enterprise as a means of
collecting information to assist in the investigation of the organization's illegal activities. Therefore, such organizations often
take the form of groups or cells of friends, associates, and family members who trust one another because they have common
geographic origins, ethnic backgrounds, language, or beliefs.*

*The identification of a drug trafficking organization or
other organized crime group is based upon one or more factors—the source of the drugs trafficked; the geographic
reach of the organization; the location of the individual(s)
who receive and control the proceeds of the organization's
activities; or the race, national origin, or group membership
(as in outlaw motorcycle gangs) of the individuals who
direct and control the organization. For instance, the term
"Mexican Drug Trafficking Organization" (DTO) may
refer to a drug trafficking organization engaged in the international distribution of drugs from Mexico and whose*

members are of Mexican descent, or one in which drug traf-
ficking proceeds are directed to individuals who are located
in Mexico. Likewise, "Eurasian" or "Asian" organized crime
groups refer to organizations that are directed and con-
trolled by individuals from a specific geographic area or who
share a common culture of origin.

The characteristics of a particular organized crime group
have practical investigative consequences. The strategy to
combat a "Mexican DTO" is different from the strategy to
combat a home-grown organization because the former has
an international base of supply and production, and U. S.
law enforcement agencies have little or no enforcement
authority in a foreign country.

Bickford's notes again: "This structure sounds like your guys. It's usually a hierarchy with only one or two leaders to give orders. I'll bet Delgado got the cocaine from Canada—because it's closer—then filled the moose with it. What you saw was him turning that over to a local gang for distribution. He came in from the outside because the shipment was so huge. We still need to figure out the money angle. Who paid who?"

Then Bickford sent me material on the health effects of cocaine use. He had written on the top of it, "Lest we forget the cost!"

FROM THE DRUG AND ALCOHOL
RESOURCE CENTER

Cocaine is a powerfully addictive drug that is snorted, sniffed, injected, or smoked and directly affects the brain. It is also called by the street names coke, snow, flake, blow, and others. Cocaine usually makes the user feel euphoric and ener-getic. Cocaine is a strong central nervous system stimulant that interferes with the reabsorption process of dopamine, a chemical messenger associated with pleasure and movement.

Cocaine is generally sold on the street as a fine, white, crystalline powder. Street dealers generally dilute it with such inert substances as cornstarch, talcum powder, sugar, or with active drugs such as procaine (a chemically related local anesthetic) or with other stimulants such as amphetamines. Cocaine abuse and addiction continues to be a problem that plagues our nation. We now know more about where and how cocaine acts in the brain, including how the drug produces its pleasurable effects and why it is so addictive. Adults 18 to 25 years old have the highest rate of current cocaine use, compared to other age groups, presumably because it is very expensive.

Common health effects include heart attacks, respiratory failure, stroke, and seizures. Large amounts can cause bizarre and violent behavior. In some cases, sudden death can occur on the first use of cocaine or unexpectedly thereafter. Physical effects of cocaine use include constricted blood vessels, dilated pupils, and increased body temperature, heart rate, and blood pressure. The duration of cocaine's immediate euphoric effects, which include hyper-stimulation, reduced fatigue, and mental clarity, depends on the route of administration. On the other hand, the faster the absorption, the shorter the duration of action. The high from snorting may last 15 to 30 minutes, while that from smoking may last 5 to 10 minutes. . . .

Different means of taking cocaine can produce different adverse effects. Regularly snorting cocaine, for example, can lead to loss of sense of smell, nosebleeds, problems with swallowing, hoarseness, and a chronically runny nose. Ingesting cocaine can cause severe bowel gangrene . . . .

"Enough," I muttered. This was really depressing. Cocaine was bad for anyone crazy enough to take it. Despite my disgust, however, I read the last paragraph:

Cocaine is not a new drug. In fact, it is one of the oldest known drugs. The pure chemical, cocaine hydrochloride, has been an abused substance for more than 100 years, and cocoa leaves, the source of cocaine, have been ingested for thousands of years. Pure cocaine was first extracted from the leaf of the Erthroxylon coca bush, which grows primarily in Peru and Bolivia, in the mid-19th century. In the early 1900s, it became the main stimulant drug used in most of the tonics/elixirs that were developed to treat a wide variety of illnesses. Today, cocaine is a Schedule II drug, meaning it has high potential for abuse.

I had probably only scratched the surface of background information about cocaine, but I now felt a bit more clued in about what law enforcement agencies were up against. These facts also made it very clear that the gang I caught a glimpse of at the sanatorium were ruthless and would do anything to protect the cocaine they depended on to survive. I had no doubt that they would kill anyone who stood in their way.

I had almost turned the fax machine off when it suddenly started to transmit something else.

DUNCAN DELGADO PSYCHIATRIC HISTORY
PERSONAL AND CONFIDENTIAL

Subject was in and out of foster homes as a child, but then was assigned to the Illinois Adolescent Treatment Center when he was fifteen after one of the homes he was staying in burned to the ground, with the family barely escaping. There he remained under continual counseling until his eighteenth birthday. After his release and subsequent enrollment at the University of Illinois, he saw a psychiatrist weekly for four years. Later, after the woman died of an apparent heart attack at the age of forty, Delgado admitted to their longtime affair.

Throughout his years in graduate school at Harvard University, Delgado sought psychiatric help at various times, but did not see a psychiatrist on a regular basis. During that time, he was accused of inappropriate behavior by a fellow research assistant (female), but she was dismissed instead of him. He got a glowing recommendation from the dean at his first teaching post in California, despite a minor scandal when he was caught by campus police leaving the dean's home at 3 A.M. The dean's wife later committed suicide. After this incident, Delgado spent four months in a private psychiatric hospital near San Diego.

Bickford had added another notation to this report: "Can you believe this guy? I'm no expert, but he seems pretty nuts to me."

I got up from my desk and started to walk away, but the fax machine had one more tidbit from Bickford. It was a short item from a newspaper in Bellingham, Washington, near the Canadian border.

MOOSE ON THE LOOSE?

Border Patrol and RCMP officers are scratching their heads over a report they received from a tourist crossing at the remote station at Sumas, Washington at 3 A.M. yesterday. A man and wife said that they saw a man driving a pickup truck pulling a horse trailer along a remote road. Instead of a horse in the trailer, however, they swore they saw the head and antlers of a large moose sticking out of the rear door.

June 29, 2005

ecause the Corvallis Municipal Airport normally handled private planes, cargo carriers, and a few corporate jets, personnel working there must have been a bit startled when the sleek executive jet landed shortly after 7 A.M. I waited next to the small headquarters building for it to roll to a stop. The distinctive white and blue U. S. Air Force markings and aluminum body glistened brightly in the sun of the summer morning.

Paul Bickford was the first person off the plane, and he walked briskly toward me, as usual not smiling.

"Civilian clothes and an Air Force plane," I said, extending my hand. "You are really in disguise. I thought you were going to fly the Red Eye into Portland. I was surprised to get your message about this change."

"I needed to get here as fast as possible. It was the only transport I could get from where I was," he said, returning the handshake.

"And that was . . ."

"You know the drill here, Tom."

And then we both repeated what he always said: "If I told you that, I'd have to kill you."

That brought a smile to his face. "I'm really glad to see you."

"Same here, even in these unpleasant circumstances."

He seemed to be looking for something as we walked around the building and into the parking lot. "There's supposed to be a car for me here."

"Left in the dead of night by elves."

"Government elves with security clearances," he replied.

"I could have driven you around."

"I need the flexibility of my own car. This way, I can drive you. And, besides, I can remain more official."

"Are you ever unofficial, Paul?"

"Not so you'd notice."

"Is that your only bag?"

He nodded. "I travel light."

We walked to an unmarked Chevrolet, and he opened the doors with a remote control device he pulled out of his pocket. He threw his bag and a briefcase into the back seat. "I'll follow you back to town, then you can leave your car at home or on campus," he said.

"I'm staying away from campus this summer," I said. "I'm lying pretty low right now."

He nodded and got in the car. I walked quickly to my own vehicle, parked a few spaces away, and backed out. As I drove along the row of cars, he pulled in behind me. I drove out onto Airport Road and then turned left on Highway 99W for the trip into town. We arrived at my condo within fifteen minutes. I directed him into the driveway of my unit and parked next to him.

"Come in and sit down, Paul. I'll put some coffee on."

As I did that, Bickford walked around my house, looking at my books and the pictures on the walls. Then he ducked into the bathroom. By the time he emerged, I had two cups of coffee sitting on the table in my dining area.

He went to the phone and unscrewed the receiver. "Ever think you'd been bugged, Tom?"

"Not that I know of."

"I only gave this place a cursory check, and it looks clean," he replied. "But you never know."

"This whole mess is about a murder, nothing involving national security," I said.

Bickford said nothing for a while as he drank his coffee. Then, "Starbucks?"

"No, it's too bitter. I go to a place here where the guy makes up his own blends."

"You got any classical music we can turn on? Something loud."

I got up and walked over to the stereo unit in the living room and put in a CD of Tchaikovsky's *1812 Overture*. "That should do it," I said, resuming my seat at the table.

Bickford opened his briefcase and slid a folder across the table toward me. "Read this and then we will talk."

The two pages he handed me contained a summary of something called "Operation Loco Lobo." The document described how the DEA, Border Patrol, and Army Intelligence were working together to find and arrest a gang of Mexican drug smugglers who were targeting the West Coast, from California to the Washington/Canada border. The group was particularly vicious, having killed both federal agents and civilian witnesses to their crimes on both sides of the border.

"Loco Lobo. Does that have anything to do with a dog?" I asked Bickford, when I had finished reading the file.

"Yeah, it does. The leader of this band of cutthroats has a huge wolf dog that he calls Lobo, which means wolf in Spanish. Why do you ask?"

"I saw that dog yesterday."

"That confirms what I suspected after looking at those photos you sent me," he said. "The guy is definitely Jesus Maldanado. He is a big player in the drug trade. A real mean guy. Did you actually see him up close?"

"Only from a distance. But the lady who took those pictures talked to him."

Bickford gulped and almost choked on his coffee. "And lived to tell about it?"

"She did live to tell about it," I smiled. "When you meet her, you'll maybe understand why. She's pretty plucky."

Bickford shook his head. "She's very lucky to be alive. Is she a police woman or someone in law enforcement?"

"She's a 70-something-year-old grandmother and amateur painter who lives on the coast."

Bickford shook his head in amazement.

"More coffee?"

He nodded and I refilled his cup.

"You want to debrief her?"

"As soon as I can."

"I'll call her, and we can drive over to her house. It'll take about an hour and a half. Before we do that, can you tell me how this fits together with Delgado and Maxine March?"

"We think that Delgado hooked up with Maldanado somewhere along the line and acted as a middle man to get both the drugs and the illegals you saw into the U. S. I'm not sure why Maldanado needed Delgado or would cut into his own profits to pay him. I presume Ms. March has disappeared because Delgado decided she knew too much about what he was doing. It is a bit murky right now."

"But you told me about the sanitarium on the phone, like you knew she was there."

"A wild guess. We had some satellite photos of that area and some intercepts that seemed to pinpoint that place as an area of possible illegal activity. I mean, it's been abandoned for years, then suddenly lots of people are hanging around the place. I figured I would steer you there to . . ."

"Keep me busy and distracted," I said. "I guess you know me better than I thought you did."

"I know you usually go off half-cocked and get into messes I have to get you out of," he said, breaking into a rare smile. "In this case, since I didn't have the time at that moment to delve into this myself, I figured you'd nose around until I could get here. You might even turn up something useful, and you sure as hell did."

"I'll take that as a compliment," I laughed, trying to squelch the feeling of pride I had that someone like Bickford would trust me to do anything, given my occasional bungling in the past. "But I still don't get why this is a matter for an Army Special Ops guy like you. This is drug smuggling."

Bickford got up and walked to the stereo unit. He picked another CD and inserted it. Soon, the lush tones of Beethoven's *Ninth Symphony* were filling the room very loudly. "I love the 'Ode to Joy' movement," said Bickford, as he stopped to listen. "Really outstanding."

We both were quiet for a few minutes as we let the music distract us from the serious business at hand.

"We have had a report from two informants that Maldanado may be about to smuggle more than drugs across the border," he continued. "He may have raised the ante quite a bit. Along with the drugs, he may be about to bring in two high-level terrorists from Afghanistan."

ickford wouldn't say anything more about the terrorists. I was surprised he had told me as much as he did. In our brief friendship, he had usually refused to discuss any of his work.

On the drive to the coast, we talked only about mundane things. He was a graduate of West Point and had been in the military for twenty years, largely in intelligence or Special Operations work. I also learned that he had been born in Colorado, loved the outdoors, and had never married, mostly because of his work. We had more in common than I thought.

I had called Pat Thompson from home and arranged us to drop by her house as soon as we could get there. We drove into her driveway just before noon.

"You start the conversation and get us to where we need to go," he said. "You know her and I do not. I don't want to scare her, but I do need to warn her about what she could be mixed up in."

Pat opened the door soon after I rang the bell. "Hello, Tom," she said with a big smile on her face. "And you must be the mysterious Paul Bickford Tom has told me so much about."

Bickford glared at me, but I shrugged him off. I hadn't told her anything about Bickford except his name and the fact that he was a friend. She had only added her own style of friendliness to those meager facts.

"Please come in." She stepped aside, and we walked into her spacious living room. Even Bickford seemed impressed with the view of the ocean and Cascade Head to the north.

"A lot of that is owned by a land conservation organization and is preserved. There are some spendy houses up there and an art school and even a herd of elk," I said, pointing at the Head.

He nodded. "I feel rested already," he replied.

"Please sit down, gentlemen," said Pat. "I've fixed us some lunch." She walked into the adjoining kitchen and began to place bowls and plates on the counter.

"Can I help you?" I called to her.

"No, I'm all set. I think it's ready. Come on in."

Bickford and I found a large green salad, a pasta salad, French bread, and glasses of iced tea waiting for us on the table.

"Sit down and help yourselves," she said, motioning for us to take the seats on either side of the table, while she sat between us at the end.

Bickford and I both filled our plates and started eating immediately.

"Very good, Pat. Thanks," I said.

"I don't get to eat home cooking very much, Ms. Thompson," Bickford added. "This is really delicious."

"Paul is used to eating MREs, Pat. Not really food."

"MREs?" she asked.

"Meals Ready to Eat," he explained. "Highly concentrated stuff that fills you up, but isn't all that good. In the Army, we call them 'Meals rejected by everyone'."

Pat and I both laughed. I was pleased to see that Paul was being less grim than usual—I didn't want him to scare Pat with what we were about to discuss.

"I thought you were going to go to Portland with your daughter," I said. "I was surprised to find you here."

"I know I said I would, but she had to go out of town and I decided I might just as well stay here if I was going to be alone there anyway," she said.

"I told Paul what happened to you, and I showed him your photos. In fact, that's why he came out here to talk to you in person." I nodded to Bickford, and he finished chewing some bread before speaking.

"Ms. Thompson, I know you kind of stumbled into this situation and are a bit bewildered by what you saw. I want to say that your photos were outstanding, and they may help us bring some pretty bad guys to justice. I know you put yourself at risk by taking the photos, and I thank you very much for doing so."

Pat squared her shoulders and smiled, looking very proud of herself. "It all happened so quickly, I didn't know what was going on until it was over."

Bickford's smile vanished. "But you've got to know that you put yourself at great risk by what you did. You could easily have been killed. In fact, I am very surprised that you weren't killed when those men found you at the sanitarium. These men are trained killers, all of them."

"Except Duncan Delgado," I interrupted.

"Yeah, we aren't sure what he is yet," said Bickford. "At any rate, I want you to promise me that you will leave this house today and go somewhere you consider safe. If you wish, I will see that you are transported to a government safe house. I don't know if that is necessary, but you need to understand that these men will stop at nothing to keep you from revealing what you learned during your brief time out there in the forest."

Pat's face went from smiling to frowning, to looking scared.

I reached over and patted her hand. "It will be all right," I said. "Paul will protect you until this is over."

"I know you think I am a meddling old woman, Tom, but I really was trying to do the right thing. I have such a good life here. I don't want it to end by being foolish."

"That's all I need to hear," said Bickford. "I'll see that you are protected. If you have a place to go, I'll get you there and see that you are guarded."

"Maybe my daughter's house. She has a different last name."

"Good idea," I said.

"Okay, now," continued Bickford, "why don't you tell me everything that happened to you out at the Ocean Springs Sanitarium."

And that she did for the next half hour. Most of it I already knew and had briefed Bickford on. He took notes as she spoke calmly of her very eventful day in the woods.

"So, why do you think they treated you so gently?" he asked, when she finished telling her story.

"I think he must have had a grandmother he loved very much, I really do," she said. "Maybe it was the Latin respect for elders, I can't be sure. But Señor Maldanado . . . was that his name?"

Bickford nodded.

"Señor Maldanado made sure I was fed and had water. He also did not tie my hands and feet or put the gag in my mouth until near the end. Maybe it would have been different if he had known I had my camera. But he did not have me searched, so he never discovered it."

"You are very lucky in that regard too, Ms. Thompson . . ."

"Please call me Pat."

"Okay, Pat. Knowing about the camera might very well have set him off. You see, he would have viewed it as a betrayal of his good treatment of you. I'm glad he didn't find it because it gives us the only proof that Jesus Maldanado and his gang are operating openly in the U. S. And we have a hint at the means of transport for the drugs we think he is smuggling into this country."

"You mean the moose?" she said.

"Ah, yes, the moose," said Bickford, smiling. "That is the most unusual way to smuggle drugs any of our people have ever encountered. Pretty bizarre."

"And we have Duncan Delgado to thank for that little twist in the story," I added.

"Your testimony can put him at the scene with the drug gang," said Bickford. "It will be important."

A look of terror crossed Pat's face. "You mean I will have to testify to this in court?" She started to look scared again. I patted her hand.

"You should probably plan on it, although I'm sure our attorneys would try to avoid calling you," Bickford said.

I wouldn't bet on that, I thought to myself. Federal prosecutors can be pretty ruthless and uncaring when it comes to handling their cases. Pat's age and fear would play no part in any decision to put her on the stand.

"I . . . I . . . I'm a good citizen," she sighed. "I'll do what I have to do."

"I know you will," Bickford said, unsmilingly, but not unkindly. "Is there anything else you want to say? I don't have any more questions."

"No, I think that is about it."

"I guess you got your car back?" I asked.

"Yes, that nice Mr. Pearl brought it for me the next day, with a very polite young Mexican man."

"Raymond Pearl is my attorney's investigator and the kid works for him, too," I said to Bickford. "I dropped Pat off after we left Ocean Springs."

Bickford nodded at me and glanced discretely at his watch. I took the hint.

"Can we help you with the dishes, Pat?" I said, rising from the table.

"No, no. I can get it." She turned to Bickford. "Will I be leaving here soon?"

"Yes, as soon as I can arrange it. You should pack what you need right now and then wait at maybe a neighbor's house until I can get you picked up. I don't want you to stay here any longer. Just in case. I know I have alarmed you, but I needed to emphasize how desperate these men are. Do you understand?"

"I have not lived all these years without picking up some common sense, Mr. Bickford," she said, looking at him directly. "In spite of the foolish decision I made to go out to that place alone."

Bickford seemed embarrassed. "I didn't mean to be condescending."

"You weren't. Let me just clear the table and put these dishes in the dishwasher. My cleaning lady will straighten up when she comes tomorrow."

I grabbed some dishes and carried them to the kitchen. Bickford moved into the living room and stepped out onto the deck, then pulled out his cell phone and punched in some numbers.

"Show me how to work this, and I'll put the rest of the dishes in," I said. "You need to pack a bag."

Pat poured soap into the container on the door and rolled in the two shelves that were now full of dirty dishes. She rotated the lever and punched the START button.

"Done. I'll go get my things," she said.

* * * * *

An hour later, Bickford and I were driving up the Siletz River highway heading into the Coast Range. Bickford had called the FBI office in Portland and arranged for Pat Thompson to be picked up at her neighbor's house two doors away. She would be housed under guard in her own condo or at a government safe house in Portland until this case was settled and her status as a witness was decided.

"You were right, she is one plucky lady," he said. "She will make a great witness—if we can keep her alive."

"You have your doubts about that?" I asked. "God, I'd hate to have anything happen to her. I got her into this. I couldn't live with myself if she was killed."

"These are ruthless guys, Tom. I'm really astounded that they didn't kill her on the spot."

We drove in silence for five minutes or so.

"Look at it this way, Tom. You saved her life by getting her out of there. We'll try to keep her safe. I really mean that."

As Bickford stopped at the intersection with the road that would eventually take us to the sanitarium, I asked him to pull off the road so I could check my phone messages.

"I haven't done this all day."

I punched in the proper codes and listened. Nothing too pressing until I heard the third message.

"This is Maud Baxter at the museum. I think you need to come over here. Something very big has turned up that you're going to want to see."

ell me once again why we are driving to campus before we go to that sanitarium," Bickford said, with irritation in his voice. "I thought that was going to bring us closer to getting Maldanado and Delgado."

We had turned onto Highway 20 from the road to Siletz and were heading east through a landscape that alternated between beautiful fir-covered mountains and devastated clear-cut areas that look like an atom bomb had hit them.

"I think the missing moose has returned to the museum," I said. "The one in the photos. That's how the cocaine was brought in. You need to examine it closely."

"For what reason? To take fingerprints off the antlers?" scoffed Bickford.

"I don't see why everyone makes fun of moose," I said, disgustedly. "If it was a horse or even a deer, your reaction would be very different."

"Seriously. I know I have to get the lab guys on it. In the

meantime, let me know when we're there." Saying that, Bickford got into a more comfortable position and promptly went to sleep. I've always marveled at some people's ability to take power naps. It had never worked for me.

We drove in silence the rest of the one-hour drive to Corvallis. I parked in the lot next to the museum and tapped Bickford on the shoulder.

"Paul, we're here."

He awoke with a start and then stretched and yawned. "Wow, I was really conked out. I don't normally get a lot of sleep, so I try to catch a few winks whenever I can. You ought to try it, Tom. It works wonders."

"But not when I'm driving, I guess."

We got out of the car, and I pointed the way to the side door where I had entered on my previous visit.

"The museum's been closed for a while, so we've got to get in over here."

I expected to have to pound on the door to gain entry, but it swung open at my first tap on it. We stepped in and stood for a moment in the long hall that led to the various storage rooms.

"Maud," I said.

No response.

"MAUD BAXTER."

I looked at Bickford, and he shrugged.

"Maybe she's working in another area."

He and I started walking down the hall. In a few seconds, I heard some rapid steps from above and then a door slam.

"MAUD, IT'S TOM MARTINDALE," I was still shouting. "WE'RE DOWN HERE IN THE LOWER HALL."

While I was trying to locate Maud Baxter, Bickford had started looking into each of the storage rooms.

"What a lot of junk," he said, as I joined him.

"Like antique dealers always say, one man's junk is another man's treasure," I replied. "This stuff represents the history of this area—and of the university."

"Yeah, yeah, yeah," he snorted. "I guess I've never been an acquirer of 'stuff.' I move around too much for that."

"Do you even have a home somewhere?"

Bickford didn't answer my last question. He had opened the door of the last storage area on the left.

"Tom, you'd better come down here."

I walked to the doorway and looked in, somewhat reluctantly because of the tone of his voice.

Maud Baxter's body was lying at the foot of the moose, her arms and legs covered with slash marks and arrayed in four directions like the points of a compass.

gulped. "Poor Maud. She was really a great person. Very dedicated to this place." Bickford's training kicked in, and he walked over to the body and checked for a pulse.

"She's gone," he said. "I'm sorry, Tom. He touched her face gently. "I'd say she hasn't been dead long."

"We probably surprised the killer," I said. "I mean, the footsteps and the slamming door."

"Yeah, too late to follow up on that lead," he said. "Whoever it was is long gone by now. I suppose it was one of two guys— Maldanado or Delgado. They brought back the moose, and she saw them or something like that."

"Not much doubt. That bastard. He doesn't care who he hurts."

By this time, Bickford was using his phone to report Maud's death.

We were both standing in the hall as several members of the state police unit assigned to campus walked in the door ten minutes later. I braced myself for a confrontation with Angela Pride, the old girlfriend I blamed for my arrest.

"Colonel Bickford, nice to see you again," she said, not bothering to look in my direction. "I guess I should be surprised to see you here, but, then again, I have learned never to be surprised at anything Tom Martindale is involved with."

"Hello to you, too, Angela."

She ignored me and kept talking to Bickford. "Take me in and tell me what happened."

She and Bickford stepped into the storage room, but one of the officers with her barred my entry.

"Police personnel only, sir," he said, looking at Angela for confirmation of his action, which she gave with a slight nod of her head.

With no legal leg to stand on to accompany them, I shrugged and sat down as close to the door as I could. From here, I could hear snatches of their conversation from inside the room. I pretended to consult my date book, but continued to eavesdrop.

" . . . got a call about this . . ."

"Not aware . . . missing. Why wasn't . . . informed. God damn, Tom, he's . . ."

". . . be a big pain in the ass, but I've always thought . . ."

". . . let him dictate what I do . . ."

". . . major drug investigation. . . . Used to smuggle cocaine into this . . ."

"That's a novel way to . . ."

". . . Delgado may be . . ."

"Tom blames him for everything except the Kennedy assassination."

I heard Bickford laugh. "And he's working on that link now."

Thanks a lot, Paul, for your support, I thought.

". . . Maud Baxter involved?"

"Tom was asked . . . find missing moose and then . . ."

". . . always stumbles into things and then tries to big foot it and usually . . . mess."

My face was getting hot, and I wanted to burst into the room and confront them both. I started to stand up and looked at the officer standing on the other side of the door who had heard everything I had heard. He looked as if he read my thoughts and shook his head. I sat down and went back to a serious look at my date book.

Paul and Angela soon came out of the storage room. For a few minutes, he talked on his cell phone; Angela and I waited until he ended the call.

"So, what did you two great minds come up with, other than to conclude that I did not kill Maud Baxter," I said, snottily.

"Tom always tries to make himself the center of things," Angela said to Bickford without so much as a glance at me.

I addressed him directly, too. "Sometimes I'm put at the center of things on trumped up charges and get hauled into jail without cause and without explanation. And sometimes the people who do that to me should be ridden out of law enforcement on a rail or some less commodious means of conveyance."

"Enough!" said Bickford, putting both hands up in front of him. "Give it a rest."

Angela and I exchanged dirty looks, but kept quiet.

At that moment, Valerie Pitt burst through a door at the other end of the hall and walked quickly toward us.

"What is going on here?" she said. "I'm Dr. Pitt, assistant director of the museum. What is the meaning of this intrusion?"

"Tell the lieutenant that Dr. Pitt worked with Maud Baxter in running the museum. She was her second-in-command," I said.

"Forgive me, professor, but I really ran this place," she said haughtily. "Miss Baxter is only a figurehead who had no academic credentials of any . . ."

Angela stepped forward. "Please sit down, Dr. Pitt." She led the small woman to the chair I had just vacated.

"What has happened?" Pitt asked, looking ready to pummel anyone who defied her supposed authority any further.

"I am sorry to tell you that Miss Baxter has been found dead inside this room. We are beginning a homicide investigation."

At first, Pitt looked confused, then promptly fainted, her fall stopped by the officer who had kept me under control earlier.

"Take her where she can rest, Ted," ordered Angela. The officer followed her order and carrying Dr. Pitt, disappeared through the door at the end of the hall.

Bickford acted as if nothing had happened and turned to me. "Lt. Pride will take over this investigation and keep me informed if she turns up evidence linking Miss Baxter's death to my drug case against the Mexicans."

"What about Duncan Delgado?" I shouted. "You got the hots for him, Angela? Why are you always protecting him?"

"That goes over the line, Professor Martindale, even for you! You need to keep your big mouth . . ."

"ENOUGH!" Bickford was shouting now, and I guess I didn't blame him.

I held up my hands and backed away from the two of them. "I'm outta here. I don't want to get into a shouting match with you, Angela. If you need to ask me any questions about this, call my attorney, Lorenzo Madrid. His office is in Salem and his number's in the phone book." I walked to the door and heard Bickford quietly say something like, "I'll work on him" or "I'll talk to him."

We were almost to the car before Bickford said anything. "That went well," he said with a smile.

By this time, we had long since missed lunch, and I was hungry. I convinced Bickford to drive into downtown Corvallis so we could get something to eat. I took him to a relatively new place on the Willamette River where they served good Reuben sandwiches, among other things. After we had both ordered, I broke the silence.

"I know you think I am pig-headed and brash. That I run around half-cocked, deliberately butting into things I should leave to people who know what they're doing."

He said nothing as he dipped a piece of bread into the olive oil/balsamic vinegar mixture on the plate beside him. He chewed the bread carefully, while I plunged ahead to say what was on my mind. I had never learned that it is sometimes best to keep quiet and not fill the void in conversation with idle chatter.

"Angela was a good friend—a close friend—and she really let me down. She should have given me some kind of warning that she was going to arrest me. I think she was jealous of Maxine. I think she deliberately . . ."

"Tom, Tom. Calm down. I think she was conflicted about what to do, but as a law enforcement person, she had to do her duty so she did what she did."

"I don't buy that! She could have helped me! We were close!"

"The fact that you slept together is beside the point," he said. He paused while the waiter served our food.

"Anything else?" asked the young man.

We both shook our heads.

"Enjoy."

"Angela's a police officer, sworn to uphold the law," he continued, his mouth full of corned beef. "In any conflict between the law and other people—no matter who those other people are—the law has to win."

"Yeah, yeah, yeah!" I ate my sandwich and drank some iced tea.

Bickford finished his food and pushed the empty plate away. "That was great. Sometimes I forget to eat." Then he got up and walked to the dessert case and spoke to the waiter on the way back to the table.

"I'm having some of that chocolate cheesecake. You want something, Tom? The government's paying."

I shook my head. "No thanks, don't tempt me."

The waiter arrived with the cheesecake, and Bickford started gobbling it up at a furious pace.

"You know, Paul, I don't think I've ever seen you eat before, much less relax."

"In Special Ops, we are taught not to eat much, unless it's insects and rodents." He smiled and finished the dessert, moistening his fingers to pick up the few remaining crumbs on the plate. I finished my salad and drank some more tea.

"So, where do we stand on things? What do I need to do? What are you going to do?"

Bickford pulled out a small notebook and tore out a page, which he began to write on with a silver pen. He pushed it in front of me.

"As we say in the Army, 'listen up.' This situation has a number of strands to it. First, we've got drug smuggling, specifically cocaine. Maldanado's bringing it into Oregon and Washington. He's already got California covered. For some reason, he's brought your favorite biologist, Duncan Delgado, into it. Delgado used the hollowed-out moose to transport the cocaine. Thanks to you, we know where the moose is, but we don't know where the cocaine is—and there is a lot of it. When it gets to the streets—if it isn't already there—it will ruin a lot of lives. By the way, I arranged for the moose to be picked up and taken to Portland for testing. We need to go over that baby for any evidence we can find."

"You were setting that up on the phone before?"

"I was, yes. As for your friend Delgado, we still need to nail him on trafficking in illegal migrants and for using them—or planning to use them—in dangerous and unlawful research."

"The Ebola virus work."

"Yeah. I imagine we can use that woman you found at the sanitarium as a key witness to that."

"Maria. Lorenzo has her tucked away safely in Portland. Could we try to help her get a green card when this is all over?"

"I can't promise, but I'll do my best for her," he smiled, then added, "That leaves the other missing piece."

"Maxine March."

"Your old love. She is our key witness against Delgado."

"And my ticket out of jail. If I prove for certain that she is alive, my case goes away."

"Yes, definitely." Then his cell phone rang. "Bickford." He got up, placed some cash on the table, and walked out the front door, listening intently as he walked across the street to the riverfront park.

I finished my iced tea and signaled for the check. After I had paid, I walked out the door and crossed the street to the park, being careful to sit on a bench far away from Bickford, who had stopped in the middle of the bike path next to the river bank. I closed my eyes and basked in the warmth of the summer sun. It felt good on my beat-up body. A shadow cut off the sun.

"There's been a slight change of plans," said Bickford. "I've got to get up to Portland to go to a meeting about Maldanado. We think we know where he is, but I've got to be there in case we find him. We think he's got some information I need for another investigation. I shouldn't tell you this, but his little operation might have brought in more than drugs in the past few months."

"Those terrorists you mentioned?"

Bickford didn't say anything, but his silence confirmed the answer.

"I need you to do something for me, Tom. I need you to go back to the sanitarium to meet a forensics team and tell them exactly what happened the other day when you saw what went down with Maldanado and Delgado and the rest of the gang. We need evidence, and only you can show them where to collect it."

"Sure, I'll do it. Tell me where and when."

Bickford looked at his watch. "Kinda late now, but we've got a couple more hours of daylight. How about you driving to the sanitarium, and I'll have them meet you. I talked to the DEA agent in charge of this case, and he said he'd send a team by helicopter. He checked a map and thinks he can land right on the grounds of that place. I'm sorry we can't go there together. I like creepy places."

"That's okay," I said. "But I'm sorry not to be able to give you the grand tour of that place. It is really something."

"I'll drop you off so you can get your car," he said. "Promise me this, Tom: wait for the DEA crew to arrive and don't do your usual headlong rush."

I pointed at myself mockingly. "Me, get into trouble? You've got to be talking about someone else."

ecause I was on the east side of the Coast Range, I would have to get to the sanitarium the way I did the first time I went there. Without a four-wheel-drive vehicle—like Lorenzo's Jeep—that meant another drive to Valsetz and a hike on foot to the sanitarium. On the way to Valsetz, I called my attorney to fill him in on the developments, which were now happening quickly. Unfortunately, he was out of the office. I left him a detailed message and told him where I was going.

"So I may have this all wrapped up when I see you again," I said in closing. "If I do, I hope we can run this by the judge and get my name cleared."

I ended the call as I got out of the car and headed into the forest.

Even though I knew the way because of my earlier trek through this area, it was still hard to walk. The warmth of the summer sun had caused the brush to grow over the path. Because I didn't have anything to cut with but my small pocketknife, I

181

had to keep pulling on plants to get through. It was slow going and took twice as long as before.

It was nearly dark when I reached the bottom of the hill, below the Ocean Springs buildings. As I stopped to rest, I thought I saw a brief flash of light from above, but decided that my eyes were playing tricks on me in the fading twilight. It was nearly 8:30. I strained to hear the roar of the helicopter engine, but all was silent. I drank some of the water I carried and then rested.

After about fifteen minutes, I started climbing up the steep embankment. Here and there, I lost my footing and almost fell twice. Before long, my clothes were covered with the dust I was creating with each step. After a while, I decided that mud might be preferable.

I reached the top and walked over to the wide veranda that adjoined the building. As I sat down in one of the chairs, a breeze from the ocean caused me to shiver. As usual, I was not prepared and had no coat. After all, it was summer and who needed a coat?

More listening gave me nothing to hear but the faint rustling of the trees high above in the forest surrounding the buildings. I got up and decided to wait inside where it would be warmer.

I circled the sanitarium and went in the end door. It was pitch black in the lower hall, so I turned on my flashlight. As I walked toward the main lobby, the skittering beam caught a kaleidoscope of images: damaged furniture, discolored walls, faded pictures, and a lot of cobwebs.

The lobby was brighter, with the remaining sunlight coming in through its many windows. I sat down on one of the big leather chairs. Once expensive, it now had big holes in its fabric and the stuffing was hanging out. There was a fortune here in oak bookshelves and file cabinets, let alone the dishes, flatware, and cooking utensils in the dining room and kitchen, plus all the old medical equipment. I wondered if it would ever be sold or just be left to lie here and deteriorate.

"Tom."

Someone was calling my name, or was I dreaming? I walked to the window and looked out. Nothing but trees beyond the grounds of the sanitarium. I walked to the bottom of the stairway and listened again, but heard nothing. I returned to the lobby so I could go out and guide the DEA guys when the helicopter landed—if it ever did.

"Tom. Help me."

The voice was louder than before and more insistent. I had to check it out, helicopter or no helicopter. The others would find me once they landed.

I walked up the stairs to the second floor, but saw and heard nothing. I knew I was tired, but didn't think I was hearing voices.

"Tom, I need you."

The voice was unmistakable. It was Maxine March.

"Maxine. MAXINE."

I was shouting now and running down the hall to the psychiatric unit where I had found signs of her before.

"Where are you?"

The door to the unit was slightly ajar, and I pushed it open and stepped inside, in time to see a flash of white flit from one side of the hall to the other at the end. I ran there. Nothing.

I walked into the end room on the right. Although it was empty, I noticed a small dark object on the small table beside the sagging bed. I walked over and picked it up: a sophisticated cassette recorder whose message was timed to sound out at regular intervals.

"Tom. Help me."

I jumped back as the disembodied voice of someone I cared about rang out.

"Tom. I need you."

In my disgust and disappointment, I threw the recorder out the broken window. When it landed on the ground below, the voice kept speaking, only now more faintly and repeatedly.

"Tom. I need you, need you, need you."

I covered my ears and sat down against the wall.

"A man in your station in life should not give in to temper tantrums. What would your students think? But do you even have any students, now that you are in disgrace?" Duncan Delgado stood over me with a gun in his hand. "Get up and sit on the bed."

"You've turned yourself into quite a mass murderer," I said, more angry than fearful of this man who had ruined my life since the day I first met him over a year before.

A smile crossed his face, as if he took my taunt as praise. An award-winning biologist, an award-winning killer. He'd take any accolade he could get.

"Me, a killer? Surely you jest, Martindale." He relaxed a bit and lit a cigarette. He did not lower the gun, however.

I pressed on because I had a lot to get off my chest, no matter what the consequences. He'd kill me anyway, so why not vent for a while? "Well, let's see, there's that poor sap Hector Morales and Maxine March—or the woman you tricked police into thinking was Maxine, Margarita Santoro. I bet you didn't even know her name, did you? And, more recently, we can't forget Maud Baxter at the museum."

"I don't know what you're talking about," he smiled.

"That's not counting the poor illegals who probably died on the trip up here to take part in your research on Ebola fever. Did you get a chance to inject them and watch them bleed?"

Delgado did not flinch, but said, "Some must be sacrificed in the name of medical science. All great scientists have known that.

We do what we do to benefit mankind, but choices must be made along the way. We all benefit in the end." He looked dreamily out the window behind me, as if contemplating the awards ceremony for the Nobel Prize he had all but awarded to himself.

"Satisfy my curiosity, Delgado. How did you do everything you've done in the past year or so. And why did you pick me as the scapegoat?"

He smiled again. "I'll answer the last question first. It was so easy to turn all suspicion onto you. All I needed was to plant your faculty card on the body and, for good measure, add a bit of blood on it. You were so prominent on campus, I knew your fall from grace would take the heat off me. Plus, you were poking around into things that were none of your business. Anyone ever tell you that you are an asshole at times?"

"It has been said, yes," I said.

"A smart asshole, I'll give you that. And a relentless one. You figured out what I was doing at the lab and even saw my first group of research subjects. Am I right? You were there that night?"

I nodded.

"And you found this place? God, I could not believe it when I heard you were messing around here. How'd you find it?"

"I saw a painting in the window of a gallery in Newport and tracked down the painter. She told me where it was."

"Oh yes, that old woman I found here. Who is she?" asked Delgado.

"I never got her name. Probably from out of state."

"I let her go because I thought as much. My friend here was not so sure—and still isn't."

At that moment, Jesus Maldanado stepped into the room, his wolf dog at his side, snarling and lunging toward me. "*Bastante!*" he shouted, and the dog sat down docilely. Turning toward me, he said, "You have given us many sleepless nights, *señor*. You are a big pain in the ass. And you know what we do to big pains in the ass? We remove them by lancing the boil." Maldanado laughed loudly. "And you look like a big boil to me. Right Lobo?" The dog looked up into his master's eyes and started wagging his tail.

"If you're going to kill me anyway, can I ask some questions?"

Delgado looked at Maldanado, and the big man nodded his assent.

"How did the two of you get together? I mean, a biologist and a drug dealer do not normally hang out together."

"We are half-brothers," said Delgado. "Same mother, different fathers. We had not seen one another since we were kids. Jesus contacted me when I made a trip to our home village in Mexico two years ago. I took Maxine on the trip to see my old stomping grounds. It was a misguided attempt on my part to save our marriage. After we met, Jesus asked me to help him and I decided to do it—for him and for me."

"The money from the drugs was to pay for your research."

Delgado nodded.

"And the moose?"

"Only a unique means of transportation," he smiled.

"My brother is a smart man—in some ways," said Maldanado. "He thought of that, and it was brilliant."

"Once it had served its purpose, I made sure it was returned," added Delgado.

"But why'd you have to kill Maud Baxter? She was a great lady who was just trying to get her museum open."

"That is the second time you have accused me of killing Maud," Delgado said. "I did not kill her and know nothing about it. Jesus?"

The big man shook his head.

"I don't believe you, but it doesn't matter what I believe. The police think you did it, and that's good enough for me. You've killed so many people that maybe you even forgot such an insignificant death."

Delgado shrugged his shoulders. "It is of no importance to me what you think or if you believe me. You will soon be beyond caring about Maud Baxter or much of anything else."

Delgado motioned for me to get up and I did. Maldanado and Lobo stepped aside to let me follow Delgado out into the hall. As I passed the dog, he took a nip at me, with a few snarls thrown in for good measure.

I stopped in the hall. "Before we proceed to whatever you're going to do to me, I want to ask you about Maxine. I need to know what happened to her."

"Oh yes, my beautiful wife."

"She's one fine piece of ass," said Maldanado.

Delgado gave his half-brother a dirty look, but said nothing to him. Instead, he answered my question. "I forgot to say before that your obvious interest in her was another reason I felt I needed to get rid of you. A man does not like another man to go sniffing around his wife . . ."

"Ex-wife," I said. "She said you'd been divorced for years."

"Not in my heart was she an 'ex'," he said, putting his hand over his heart.

"What a bunch of crap!" I shouted. "You never treated her well. You subjected her to years of physical and mental abuse. You could not stand to see her happy. You could not stand to see her have a career or a life of her own. You could not stand to see her turn to someone else for comfort and love! She told me how bad you were in bed. How do you like that, Mr. Latin *Macho* Man?"

At that, Delgado hit me hard with the handle of his gun, and I fell to my knees. I could feel blood running out of the corner of my mouth and a tooth fell onto the floor. Smelling blood, Lobo lunged at me and Maldanado allowed him to get close enough to sink his teeth into my arm. More blood.

I pulled a handkerchief out of my pocket and dabbed at my mouth and my arm, but it didn't do much good. Delgado motioned for me to head down the hall. We walked down the main stairway and into the lobby.

"Over that way," he said, directing me toward what I remembered was the tub room and the hot springs.

I could see the steam seeping out from under the door even before we got to it. Maldanado and Lobo walked ahead of us, and he opened the door. I stepped in and Delgado followed, nudging me in the back with the gun as a reminder that he had it.

When I had seen the tubs the week before, they had been filthy. Now, two of them were clean, with water from the hot springs pouring into them from spigots. High above both tubs were the heavy canvas slings that were used many years ago to lower the patients into the high temperature baths. I had no doubt now as to how Delgado planned to get rid of me.

"Ever hear of getting squeaky clean, Martindale?" Delgado said with a laugh. "You'll soon be that way—soft like a baby's bottom, but maybe all shriveled up like an old man. All of you will be shriveled up. But let's see what you've got to shrivel." Both he and Maldanado laughed. "Take off your clothes!"

When I did not move, Maldanado used his knife to cut off my shirt from behind. The point was so sharp, it slid right through the fabric. I quickly took off my pants and shoes and socks.

"Take off your shorts and your T-shirt," said Delgado. "We need to get a good look at this magnificent package you think Maxine was so in love with."

I complied, but tried to cover my private parts with my hands, to no avail—Maldanado let Lobo take a nip at my hands, so I moved them away. I stood there facing both of them, feeling as vulnerable as I had ever felt in my life.

Both of them stared at my penis, laughing and making rude gestures as to its size.

"*Pequeno, muy pequeno,*" said Maldanado. He held up two fingers not very wide apart.

"*Muy, muy, muy pequeno,*" added Delgado.

"Okay, okay, you've had your fun," I said. "Let me put my clothes back on. It's cold in here."

"Shut up, Martindale! What happens next will not require clothing!" said Delgado.

He handed the gun to his half-brother and pulled me toward one of the tubs. He reached up and pulled one of the slings down within reach. Then he strapped me into it so I was in a sitting position, like I was in a hammock. Then he hoisted it up so that I was suspended about six feet above the now boiling water. He tied off the sling and stepped back to admire his handiwork.

"Not bad for an amateur. I can get a job in a hospital if my teaching and research don't work out." He and Maldanado had a good laugh over that one.

"You stopped being a teacher and a researcher the minute you killed the first time," I yelled from above. "Your academic career is history. You can't do teaching or research when you're in the state pen. Those cons will love your dark Latin good looks. You'll be someone's cutie the first day. I'm sure of it!"

"Shut up, fucker!" shouted Maldanado, as he reached up with the knife and stabbed me in the rump. I cried out in pain.

"And now for the *pièce de résistance,*" said Delgado.

I watched from above as he walked into a small room at the end of the tub area and led someone toward me.

"Maxine!" I said softly, barely able to find my voice. "You are alive. Thank God."

She staggered ahead of him, barely able to focus her eyes.

"I believe you know my darling wife," Delgado sneered. "Say hello to your lover."

Then he yanked her by the hair so that her face was aimed at me, but I could tell that she was too drugged to really see me. I turned away, tears mixing with the blood that was all over my face.

I could hear Delgado saying something to her, so I looked again at them. He was removing her clothes, and she did not resist. He pulled her toward the tub next to the one I was hanging over, reached up for the sling, and pulled it down. Then he placed her arms and legs into it and hoisted her up above the steaming water.

"What a sight! Our two little love birds side by side, ready to take a bath together."

Maldanado joined him in uproarious laughter. Even Lobo wagged his tale at the joy of it all.

"Maxine," I said softly. "Can you hear me? It's Tom!"

"Shut the fuck up, *gringo!*" said Maldanado, sticking me with his knife several more times from below. At this rate, I would soon be a human colander.

"Are you ready, kids?" shouted Delgado over the roar of the water, which was now pouring in fast. Soon I couldn't see Maxine because of the steam.

I recalled reading that the patients with syphilis were submerged in water of 208 degrees. I was sure Delgado would manage to kick it up higher than that. We would probably go into convulsions and die quickly after being subjected to only a few minutes of water that hot—if we didn't drown first.

Delgado walked over to where he had tied off my sling and began to untie it. Maldanado did the same at the next tub.

"We'll do this so you hit the water together," said Delgado. "Very touching as a last tribute to your true love." He laughed again, but this time it was in a high pitch that showed the level of his madness.

"YOU ARE TOTALLY NUTS!" I yelled.

He glared at me and let loose of the slings. The force of the fall caused me to fall forward and out of the sling. As I hit the scalding water headfirst, I remember wondering if holding my breath would do me any good.

y head hit the bottom of the tub with such force that I was dazed for a moment. I did manage to hold my breath, even though I quickly began to feel the pain from the boiling water all over my body. I pawed my way to the surface in a few seconds, expecting to feel Delgado's hands on me, holding me down.

That did not happen!

I peered over the edge of the tub, rubbing my eyes to clear away the stinging sulfa water. Was the pain causing me to hallucinate? I couldn't understand what was happening.

Then I heard a loud popping sound and saw men in black suits crashing in through the doors, carrying machine guns. Delgado was lying on the floor, blood pooling around his head. Maldanado and Lobo ran and then jumped right through the large window, glass flying and bullets hitting the decaying wood around them.

I scrambled out of the tub and saw that Maxine was still suspended above the next tub. I ran over and tried to lower the sling, but my arms were burning so much that I had no control over them. They fell helplessly to my side.

"Let me help you with that, Tom," said a familiar voice. Paul Bickford removed a black hood and threw a blanket at me. "Put this around you till we get you some clothes. You look terrible."

Bickford untied the sling and let Maxine down very slowly. One of the men with him brought over a blanket, and they both wrapped it around her carefully. Bickford picked her up and carried her out the door into the hall. I followed, hobbling along on my burned feet. Then he laid her on one of the sofas in the lobby and put another blanket over her. I ran to her side.

"Maxine, it's Tom. Everything will be all right now. Just take it easy." She did not respond, but I kept saying that again and again. I cradled her head in my arms and rocked her back and forth. I kissed her on the forehead. "You are safe now, Maxie. I'll take care of you. Duncan is dead. He can't hurt you now. Just take it easy."

I was sobbing by this time, a combination of my injuries and my relief that I had finally found Maxine. We would be together now. I'd quit my job. Maybe we would leave the state which had bad memories for both of us. We'd get a new start somewhere else. My mind was a bit muddled from the shock and the pain, but I could see the future.

"Tom, this is Craig, one of our medics. He will see to your injuries and then take care of Maxine."

"No! Have him take care of Maxine first!"

The medic walked over to her and did a cursory examination. "She's been heavily sedated," he said. "I'd say she's been starved, too. There's a significant loss of body fat. Her skin is sallow and beginning to crack. I'd like your permission to transport her out of here to a hospital fast, sir."

"Granted. Let's get her on the bird and gone."

I hobbled over to her and bent down to kiss her again. She moaned softly and her eyelids fluttered.

"Maxine, it's Tom. You're safe now. Duncan is dead."

This time, she opened her eyes and looked at me. "Tom." And then her eyes closed, and she passed out again.

"We had her back—she was here," I sobbed.

Bickford raised an arm and two of his men appeared with a stretcher. They placed her on it carefully and carried it out the door. I got up to follow.

"Tom, you need to let her go for now," said Bickford, holding me back. "She's in good hands. We've got to mop things up here, and I need you to help me."

"She spoke to me. She looked at me. I need to stay with her so that I'm there when she wakes up."

Bickford gently took me by the shoulder and led me over to another sofa. I knew he was right about my condition and the need to get Maxine out of here as quickly as possible. I could hear the engines of the helicopter fire up and soon the craft thundered up and over the building.

It was too late to resist so I sat down and let the medic look me over. He whispered something to Bickford.

"What are you saying? Tell me the bad news."

"You've got burns on your arms and legs and in the groin area, sir," said the young medic. "They're probably first degree burns and are getting red, but may not blister. You were lucky you weren't in that water any longer. You'll be sore for a while, but you'll be okay." He rubbed salve on my legs and arms. "I'll let you do your . . . em . . . privates," he said.

"You'll need to keep that gun in its holster for a bit," laughed Bickford, throwing me one of the black suits.

"This 'gun' won't notice any difference," I said, smiling for the first time. I put the suit on quickly—it felt good on my beat-up body.

"Does this make me a full-fledged Ninja?" I laughed.

"Maybe a Ninja Turtle," Bickford said. "That's the intermediate step."

Bickford got up and walked over to another of his men who had just walked in from outside. He listened to the man and then turned to me.

"Damn. Maldanado got away. Dog, too. I hoped we'd nail him—he's far too dangerous to be running around, but we'll get him eventually."

Bickford walked over to the lump on the floor that had been Duncan Delgado. "At least this bastard is out of action," he said, as he threw a white sheet over him. "Let's get out of here."

July 6, 2005

A week later, everyone connected to the case waited in the conference room of the museum. Bickford had called us all together to, in his words, "tie up all the loose ends." I had not seen him since he dropped me at the hospital emergency room in Corvallis after driving me down from Ocean Springs Sanitarium. He had even seen that my car was taken to my house.

Despite my frequent calls to his cell phone, I had not heard from him at all until the day before, when he left a cryptic message about today's gathering. I did not know where Maxine was or how she was. Or if she was even alive. That was the way Paul Bickford always operated, and I accepted that. But it still drove me crazy not to know anything about Maxine, even though I knew he would protect her, no doubt better than I ever could.

I was surprised to see Lorenzo Madrid walk into the room, trailed by his investigator, Raymond Pearl. I walked over to him.

197

"So Bickford called you? I'm glad to see you."

"We need to talk," he said, shaking my hand and smiling. "You are in the clear, but I'll fill you in later."

Pat Thompson came in next, followed by her daughter. "Tom, so good to see you," she said.

"Are you in Portland or back at the coast?" I asked her.

"Sssssshhhh! I'm not supposed to say."

Hadley came in next, with the museum assistant director Valerie Pitt following her. My heart fell when Angela Pride walked in. Our last two conversations had been so harsh that I doubted our friendship had survived—nor was I sure I wanted it to. I'd be leaving here anyway, as soon as Maxine was well.

Paul Bickford was the last to arrive, probably for dramatic effect. He entered the room alone, but I could see several of his men remaining on guard out in the hallway. They had to be from Army Special Ops, although they were wearing civilian clothes.

"Good morning, ladies and gentlemen," he said, as he walked to the head of the table. "If I have inconvenienced any of you by making you come to campus today, I apologize. I decided that I needed to have all of you in the same room so I could lay out this very complicated case with some semblance of clarity. And we also have some unfinished business to take care of."

Bickford then told all of them about Duncan Delgado and his quest for fame and glory. How he had concocted the scheme to fund his research into Ebola fever by smuggling cocaine into the state with a unique means of transportation— the moose—and turning it over to his half-brother for a share of the sales profits. How he had killed anyone who had tried to stop him—like Hector Morales, the man whose charred remains I had found in the forest—and how he had faked the death of his ex-wife Maxine March, substituted the body of someone else, and then successfully pinned her murder on me. How he had kidnapped her and then tried to kill both Maxine and me at the sanitarium.

"The only person he did not try to kill was Ms. Thompson here, who he encountered at the sanitarium, but for some reason let go."

"What about Maud Baxter?" I said. "He denied killing her, but it was pretty obvious that he did it. I mean, we found her in front of the moose, so I guess she caught him bringing it back."

Bickford smiled. "Oh yes, Miss Baxter—from all accounts a great person who worked for most of her life at making this museum better. She was a victim of circumstance, but not like we thought, Tom. Isn't that right, Miss Pitt?"

We all turned to the tiny woman sitting next to Hadley Collins.

"It's DOCTOR Pitt, colonel. I am sure you will agree that titles are important. They are a sign of respect from a world which has little respect left."

"Sorry, DOCTOR Pitt," continued Bickford. "Why don't you tell us how you killed Maud Baxter."

Amid murmurs of surprise in the room, the woman did not hesitate to explain. "She was an interloper, a coarse, uneducated woman who did everything she could to undermine the academic standards I tried to set up here. I have flawless credentials and a Ph.D. She had just a high school education and thought only of preserving the legacy of her grandfather, a minor figure in the university's history. We could not possibly raise the level of excellence here with her at the helm—we need this to be a place where scholars can thrive and advance the study of Oregon history. With her in charge of the new museum, we would be the laughingstock of other universities with fine museums and world-class collections of art and manuscripts. With her in charge, the new museum would never be more than a dusty repository of moth-eaten artifacts that belong at the city dump."

"So that's why you killed her," said Bickford. "So you could take over."

Pitt nodded. "And I'd do it again, colonel. In an instant!" Pitt's eyes flashed defiantly as Angela Pride took her by the arm and led her out the door.

"God, Paul," I said. "I'd never have guessed it. That's one murder we can't pin on Delgado."

Bickford nodded. "But only that one. He has plenty of others to answer for, but he's beyond our reach now."

I shook my head, thinking of that monster lying on a gurney somewhere, very cold and very dead.

"We are nearly finished here," continued Bickford. "I have discussed with Ms. Thompson my worries for her short-term safety. She can identify Jesus Maldanado and place him at Ocean Springs, but so can you and a lot of other people. I doubt he knows her name or where she lives. We can hope that he does not remember her. To be on the safe side, however, she has agreed to go on an extended visit to her daughter in Montreal. When she returns, I hope we will have captured him."

Thompson smiled at me as I mouthed the words "I'm sorry" to her.

"Two other witnesses remain: Professor Martindale and someone most of you do not know, Maxine March, who used to be married to Duncan Delgado. For their safety, I do not plan to discuss their situations here." He looked around the room. "Does anyone have any questions?"

No one said a word.

"Then I guess we are adjourned. Thank you for coming here today."

He looked at me and then to Lorenzo Madrid, my attorney. "Please stay for a private word." When the others had gone, Bickford sat down opposite the two of us. "To use a tired cliché, I have good news and bad news."

July 7, 2005

All rise. The circuit court is now in session. The Honorable J. Betty Andrews presiding."

"Please be seated," the judge said, then looked at me and smiled. "We are here to act on a request by defendant Thomas Martindale in the matter of the death of one Maxine March. Mr. Madrid."

"Lorenzo Madrid, for the defense. I hope we can dispose of this matter fairly quickly, Your Honor, and not take up too much of the court's time."

"Objection, Your Honor. George Bates for the county. Mr. Madrid will not be making any decision about disposing of this or any case. I believe that is Your Honor's prerogative." Bates smiled and glanced at Lorenzo with a smile of one-upmanship on his face.

"You are perfectly right, Mr. Bates, but I won't know what Mr. Madrid is proposing until I hear what he has to say. Don't you agree?"

Bates quit smiling and stood up. "Yes, Your Honor. Sorry."

"Mr. Madrid, please proceed."

"Thank you, Your Honor. As you will recall, on June 22, 2005, you released my client, Thomas Martindale, on his own recognizance after I raised the point that the body found in McDonald Forest was not that of Maxine March—the woman my client is accused of killing—but someone else. We now know that it was Margarita Santoro, a resident of Mexico. You agreed with this line of reasoning, and Mr. Martindale was released from jail. Since that time, he and I and members of my staff have conducted a thorough investigation of the circumstances of this case—during which time nothing was being done by the office of the District Attorney, where Mr. Bates works."

Bates leaped to his feet. "That is an outrageous falsehood!" he shouted.

"Control your temper, Mr. Bates. I take it from your outburst, then, that your office *has* conducted an investigation into the circumstances of the death of Ms. March? The court will be happy to hear that evidence today, even before I allow Mr. Madrid to complete his presentation."

Bates looked defeated and hung his head. "We . . . I . . . er . . . decided that the burden of proving that the body was not Ms. March rested with the defense. All we knew was that we had a body and he killed her!"

Madrid was on his feet instantly. "I object, Your Honor. My client has not been convicted of any crime. Indeed, he has not even gone to trial."

Judge Andrews waved him away.

"The court does not have time to act as a referee between the two of you," she said. "We need to get on to the matter at hand: Mr. Martindale's role in the death of Maxine March."

Madrid walked to the front of the table. "Sorry, Your Honor. Thank you for the chance to present proof of my client's innocence."

He nodded to Raymond Pearl, who rolled in a metal table holding a television set and a DVD player from the back of the room. He placed it at an angle so that both the judge and those of us at the table could see the screen.

"As I was saying earlier, before the interruption . . ." Madrid shot a look of irritation toward Bates, who busied himself with the papers in front of him.

"No theatrics, Mr. Madrid," said the judge. "The court is aware of what happened. We were all here, as you will recall!"

"Sorry, Your Honor. Again, Maxine March is not dead. The victim was not Maxine March, but Margarita Santoro, a citizen of Mexico. I have the results of her autopsy, done by the Benton County medical examiner, and some records from her native country." He held up some pages and looked at them. "School records, a voter's card, and her driver's license. May I show them to the court?"

"Yes. You may approach the bench. They will be marked as exhibits." The judge took them from Madrid and handed them to her clerk, who began numbering them and entering them in her records. Madrid also gave copies to Bates. "We will assume for the sake of speeding things along that the decedent found in MacDonald Forest was Margarita Santoro and not Maxine March," she said.

Bates got to his feet. "The county is not convinced," he said.

"Duly noted. Proceed, Mr. Madrid."

"As further proof of my client's innocence, we offer you a deposition from Ms. March herself, taped yesterday at a secret location."

There were murmurs of interest from the rear of the

courtroom. Bates shifted uneasily in his chair, but said nothing.

Madrid held up a remote control for the DVD player and pressed the PLAY button. A blank screen came on first, soon followed by the words "Deposition by Maxine March, taped in Oregon on July 2, 2005, witnessed by Colonel Paul Bickford, U. S. Army; Greg Andrews, special agent in charge of the Portland office, Drug Enforcement Administration; Lee Costello, Federal Bureau of Investigation; Sgt. Edgar Williams, Oregon State Police; and June Ruggles, assistant attorney general, Oregon Department of Justice."

Quite a lot of fire power there, I thought.

The screen dissolved into the scene of Maxine sitting on a chair, facing the camera, in front of a blank white background. I was not prepared for how bad she looked. Her face, accentuated by red-rimmed eyes with dark circles under each, was bruised and without makeup. Her hair looked clean, but was badly in need of attention. She was wearing a sweatshirt that was several sizes too big and jeans that were faded and torn. I was crushed by the sight of her in this humiliated and defeated state.

She stared straight into the camera and said nothing, until someone off-camera began to ask her questions. In a voice that was at times barely audible, she told her story, beginning with her long involvement with Duncan Delgado and ending with the account of her being kidnapped by him from her apartment in Corvallis and her imprisonment by him at a number of locations in that city and also in Portland and at the sanitarium in the Coast Range. She concluded this way:

"As you can see by this tape, I am very much alive, although I am a bit bruised and very tired at the moment. I understand that a close friend of mine, Tom Martindale, has been accused of killing me. I sincerely hope that my appearance now will cause all charges against him to be dropped immediately. He never did anything to me and has always been a true friend—maybe my only friend."

With that, Maxine faded from view and the screen went dark.

Madrid pushed the STOP button on the remote, placed it on the table, and continued. "As you can see, Your Honor, and as Ms. March clearly states in her deposition, she is alive. As a result of that, we move . . ."

"Why isn't she here to speak to the court in person?" said Bates, jumping to his feet. "Why should she have special privileges?"

Judge Andrews looked at the hapless D.A. in disgust. Then, turning to Madrid, "Do you want to explain the situation to Mr. Bates?"

"I will be happy to do that, Your Honor. Ms. March had to appear by taped deposition because her life is in danger. You will note, for example, that the tape does not even specify where she was interviewed. It only says 'Oregon.' That is for her protection. She has agreed to testify in a federal investigation of Jesus Maldanado, the reputed drug lord who controls the flow of cocaine and other illegal substances into Oregon and the rest of the Pacific Northwest. Mr. Maldanado is a dangerous criminal and has killed many witnesses to his crimes in the past. Ms. March's agreement to help the government in its investigation, and any future trial of Maldanado when he is captured, puts her at great risk. As a result, she has agreed to enter the Witness Protection Program for the immediate future and, perhaps, for many years."

My heart sank at his words. I might never see Maxine again.

"The court thanks you for your explanation," said the judge. "Given the evidence presented in this courtroom this morning, I order that the charge against Thomas Martindale for the murder of Maxine March be dropped immediately."

She looked at me.

"The record will be expunged as if you were never arrested. The court apologizes, on behalf of the county and the state, that you were put through this major disruption in your life. The court wishes you good luck in the future."

I stood up as did Madrid. "Thank you, Your Honor. You have always been very fair to me."

"This court is adjourned." Saying that, the judge walked quickly through the rear door.

Bates walked over to us and held out his hand. "No hard feelings?"

"Just doing your job, I know," said Madrid.

Neither of us shook his hand, however, so he turned and walked away.

"Prick," muttered Madrid.

"Why didn't you tell me about Maxine and the Witness Protection Program?" I asked Madrid.

"I thought you knew from what Bickford told us."

I shook my head. "Will I get to see her before she leaves?"

"I'm not sure of that. I have never dealt with anyone involved in it."

He reached into his briefcase and pulled out an envelope. "I've got two letters for you. You can sit here while you read them."

The first was from Bickford who thanked me for my help and hospitality and even my friendship. Pretty gushy for him, I thought to myself. He said he'd see me when he saw me, but that he had to leave immediately for parts unknown. He did add a postscript, however:

> *I'll do my best to take care of your girl. The WPP is not in my bailiwick, but I have many friends there.*

The other letter was from Maxine. As always when I thought of her in recent days, just holding the letter brought tears to my eyes.

> *Tom—I know you are sad about where I am going. It is the best place for me under the circumstances. Odd that Duncan is still ruining my life even from the grave. But, I have survived worse than this. I will be okay. I appreciate your wonderful friendship and all you did for me. I will never forget you, but you must try to forget me. Now you need to move on with what you once called your "safe, stimulating, useful, and well-paid life."*
>
> *All my love, Maxine*